MEET THE FORTUNES!

Fortune of the Month: Grayson Fortune

Age: 37

Vital Statistics: Six-plus feet of drop-dead gorgeous in a ten-gallon hat.

Claim to Fame: He's a rodeo star so famous he goes by just "Grayson."

Romantic Prospects: Recently voted one of the most eligible bachelors in Texas. His celebrity status means he can have any woman he wants. But his family history makes him wary.

"After years on the circuit, I'm finally ready to put down some roots. Or at least a place to park some furniture. And my real estate agent, Billie Pemberton, is being very patient as I try to find the right property.

"Me, I'm feeling anything but patient. Man, if I was ten years younger, I'd... There are so many ladies I could take to my bed, but the only one I want is Billie. And I can't have her. I shouldn't want her. She's too young, too innocent for someone like me. Like it or not, I'm Jerome Fortune's son. And that means I can't be trusted..."

* * *

THE FORTUNES OF TEXAS:
THE RULEBREAKERS

Making their own rules for love in the Wild West!

Dear Reader,

Oh, I love the Fortunes of Texas. They're so wonderfully prolific! The brides. The babies. The cowboys. Wealthy. Poor. You name it, they've got it.

Most of all, whether they know it or not, the Fortunes have love. And lots of it.

Such is the case for Grayson Fortune and Billie Pemberton. He's a lot more comfortable with flirtation than commitment. She's a lot more comfortable with work than romance. But somehow, when they come together, they manage to find their way.

I hope you'll enjoy the journey!

Allison

Fortune's Homecoming

Allison Leigh

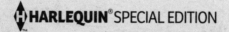

Special thanks and acknowledgment to Allison Leigh for her contribution to the Fortunes of Texas: The Rulebreakers continuity.

PLEASE RECYCLE
THIS PRODUCT IS RECYCLABLE

Recycling programs
for this product may
not exist in your area.

ISBN-13: 978-1-335-46578-8

Fortune's Homecoming

HARLEQUIN®
www.Harlequin.com

Printed in U.S.A.

A frequent name on bestseller lists, **Allison Leigh**'s high point as a writer is hearing from readers that they laughed, cried or lost sleep while reading her books. She credits her family with great patience for the time she's parked at her computer, and for blessing her with the kind of love she wants her readers to share with the characters living in the pages of her books. Contact her at allisonleigh.com.

Books by Allison Leigh

Harlequin Special Edition

Return to the Double C

Yuletide Baby Bargain
A Child Under His Tree
The BFF Bride
One Night in Weaver...
A Weaver Christmas Gift
A Weaver Beginning
A Weaver Vow
A Weaver Proposal
Courtney's Baby Plan
The Rancher's Dance

Montana Mavericks: 20 Years in the Saddle!

Destined for the Maverick

Men of the Double C Ranch

A Weaver Holiday Homecoming
A Weaver Baby
A Weaver Wedding
Wed in Wyoming
Sarah and the Sheriff

The Fortunes of Texas: The Secret Fortunes

Wild West Fortune

The Fortunes of Texas: All Fortune's Children

Fortune's Secret Heir

The Fortunes of Texas: Welcome to Horseback Hollow

Fortune's Prince

Visit the Author Profile page at Harlequin.com for more titles.

For my "forever" home.

Happy 10th.

Chapter One

"Holy cow. Is that who I think it is?"

Grayson Fortune heard the whispers start the second he walked into the office of Austin Elite Real Estate. He should have known better than to head straight there after the press conference. But going back to the hotel to change would have made him even later than he already was.

He hated being late. It was a product of his early years hustling from one rodeo to another, when being late could mean missing the event altogether. Wasted miles. Worse, wasted money.

"Ohmygawd. Is that Grayson? I just saw him on the news at noon. He's taller than I expected."

He didn't bother trying to locate where in the office the whispers came from. He just pulled off his black Grayson Gear cowboy hat and strode toward the stylish woman seated behind the reception desk. He'd had lots of practice ignoring whispers, and gave the reception-ist his usual grin.

She was probably about his mom's age, and if she rec-ognized him when she looked up at him with a friendly smile, there was nothing in her expression to say it.

"Welcome to Austin Elite." Her eyes were bright be-hind her black-framed glasses. "How can I help you?"

He heard another muffled laugh that might have been inaudible had the modern office possessed actual walls instead of a sea of glass partitions. *"I know how I'd like to help him."*

He'd asked his mother to find a real estate agent for him, and she'd set up the appointment. Otherwise he'd turn around and leave. He was used to public attention, but it was often a pain in the caboose.

"Do you suppose he's as good in the sack as the sad-dle? Imagine him tossing you down on the bed like—"

He focused harder on the friendly receptionist. "I have an appointment with Billy Pemberton. Sorry I'm late."

The receptionist consulted her computer, tapping a few keys. "Ah. There you are, Mr. Smith." She pressed a button on her phone. "Billy, your client is here." She looked up at him again with another smile. "Would you like something to drink while you wait?"

"Water would be great, ma'am."

"My pleasure." She came around the desk. "Make yourself comfortable." She gestured at the white chairs situated around an enormous world globe that sat right on the floor. Since the chairs looked like they came from outer space, he figured it made a weird sort of sense.

Two of the chairs were occupied and he took the one farthest away, nodding when the other people gave him sideways looks. Because they recognized him? Or be-cause they'd heard the chair groan when he sat on it?

More than comfort, right now he just hoped he wouldn't end up on the floor.

He also hoped the real estate agent wouldn't keep him waiting long. But considering Grayson's tardiness, he didn't have much of a leg to stand on if the guy left him cooling his heels.

He'd expected a bottle of water, but when the receptionist returned, it was with a real glass filled with water, several sliced rounds of cucumber, some narrow ribbons of green stuff threaded on a wooden swizzle stick, all topped with a curl of lemon rind. A little overdone, but a nice touch, he supposed.

If you happened to like cucumber and unidentifiable green stuff. He did not.

He took the glass. "That's real kind of you, ma'am. Thank you."

"My pleasure." She started to turn back to her desk. "Oh, there's Billy now."

He wished the globe were a coffee table, so he could have set aside the water. Instead, he stood, turning in the same direction.

The real estate agent smiled at him, approaching with a hand outstretched. "Mr. Smith, I'm so sorry for keeping you waiting."

Not a Billy.

But a *Billie*.

And what a Billie she was. From the top of her gleaming hair to the shine on her shoes, every inch was… amazing.

He juggled the glass and his hat, and stuck out his hand, anticipating the feel of her palm against his.

Bam.

No disappointment there. No, ma'am. Her skin was as soft and smooth as kid leather.

"Darlin', you weren't the one making someone wait. That's all on me."

Her rosy smile looked a little nervous and she tugged her hand free. "Don't be silly. I'm Billie Pemberton."

He wondered if his mom had chosen the attractive real estate agent deliberately.

Considering Deborah Fortune's lament lately that he needed a good woman in his life? Probably.

"Let's go back to my office, shall we?" Billie's straight hair was long and deep brown, and she tucked one side of the sleek strands behind her ear. No earrings on her earlobe. Just a tiny sparkling stud high inside her ear and two equally tiny gold rings around the top edge.

He realized he was staring, as if he'd never seen an ear before. "Yeah." He gestured with the upturned brim of his hat. "Let's get on it."

She smiled again. Definitely a hint of shyness in those appealing eyes.

Too bad she also looked like she was young enough to still be in high school. She was a real estate agent, so he knew she couldn't be *that* young, but still…

Grayson liked women. Young women. Old women. Anything-in-between women. He liked the way they thought and the way they smiled and the way they smelled.

But he didn't mess with girls. Especially ones who looked like they came complete with starry-eyed visions of picket fences and babies.

So no matter what his mom was thinking when she'd set this up, *if* she'd set this up, she was on the wrong track.

Despite all that, he told himself there was no law against appreciating how the fat silver zipper running the entire length of the back of her short white skirt worked its way up from the hem an inch as she walked ahead of him.

"He looks older than I thought he was."

The whispers started up again as the two of them made their way along a glossy hall between glass panes. Or maybe they'd never stopped. He'd quit noticing anything when Billie had smiled at him. The whispers floating in the air. The aches and pains left over from his run a few days ago in Silver City, when he'd earned nothing but a bruised rib and a face full of dirt.

Billie stepped into a cube on her right. "I'm sorry it's so tight in here." She slid onto a rolling chair at the desk. Using the toe of one tall, neon-yellow high heel, she swiveled to face the two narrow chairs positioned adjacent to her. Her sparkling eyes met his, then danced away. "Sit wherever you like."

He chuckled and dumped his hat on one of the acrylic-and-steel contraptions, then took the other. It seemed sturdier than the chairs in the reception area, at least. "D'you mind?" He lifted the water glass slightly. She didn't have anything on her desktop other than a computer screen, a stapled set of papers and a desk pad that looked like clear glass.

He had a desk that he rarely used at the Grayson Gear office. It was nowhere near as neat.

"Not at all." Her eyes danced to his. "Nasty stuff, if you ask me. I have a drawer full of plain bottled water if you prefer."

He grinned. "If you're sure you don't mind sharing."

Those eyes danced away again. "I'm sure." She moistened her soft-looking lips as she leaned over to open the bottom drawer of a short cabinet wedged into the only free corner. Beneath her silky black tank top there was a glimpse of a black bra strap, but what kept drawing his attention was the translucent creaminess of her skin.

It made him almost thirsty enough to drink the cuke crud.

She moved his water glass from the desk to the top of the cabinet, nudging aside several photo frames to make room. Then she held out the slender water bottle.

When he took it, their fingers brushed.

She quickly swiveled back to face her desk and slid her papers squarely in front of her with one hand, touching the computer screen with her other. The blank screen leaped to life, showing the same logo that was on the front door of the office. She glanced at him. "I understand you're looking for a new home."

"Yup." He waited a beat. What the hell? "Can I ask you a personal question?"

"I guess that depends," she said warily. "Will you answer my questions?"

He spread his palms. "I'm an open book, darlin'."

As he'd hoped, her expression lightened. "Somehow I doubt that. But what's the question?"

"How *old* are you?"

Fortunately, she didn't look offended. "Twenty-four. I have a college degree and I've had my real estate license for several years. I assure you, I am perfectly qualified to represent your interests and—"

He lifted his hand, cutting her off. His mom wouldn't have sent him to an *un*qualified agent. "I'm not going anywhere. I just thought I'd ask." At least she wasn't *quite* fresh out of high school. But she was still too young for him to be as attracted to her as he was, even though he appreciated her ambition. "So, let's get on with your questions."

Her lips twitched faintly. "How old are *you*?"

He couldn't help grinning. "Thirty-seven and feeling every minute of 'em, darlin'."

Her eyes twinkled. Then she looked past him for a millisecond and sat straighter in front of her computer. "All right." She slid her fingers on the glass desk pad and the logo on the screen folded away, to be replaced by a form. "Do you have an existing home now?"

"Nope."

She slid her fingers again. The screen morphed again.

"Fancy desk pad you got there." The glass clearly acted as a computer mouse pad. "How do you type?" There was no visible keyboard.

"Here." She leaned back in her chair slightly so he could see her tap the corner of the glass. The faint outline of a keyboard appeared in it. She moved her fingers across it as if she were typing on the keys, and a line of gibberish streamed across the screen. "It's cool, but it took me quite a while to get used to it." Her smile stretched, looking more than a little impish again. "Nothing but the best and cutting edge here at Austin Elite."

He shifted on the chair, staring for a second at his water bottle. Damn. She was prettier than a spring filly. He took a healthy swig from the bottle, took his time capping it, and focused on the computer screen once more. "That's what my mom said when she made the appointment here. You were the best."

"Your mother?" She'd turned her attention to the screen, as well. "Will she be living with you also?"

Not unless he could change her mind. "I doubt it. She's my business manager." He waited for Billie to ask what his business was, because she'd given no sign that she knew who he was.

"Is there anyone else you'll be consulting with on your choice of a home?"

"Like who? A wife?"

"Or a girlfriend? Boyfriend? Psychic?"

He laughed silently. "Only one I've gotta please is me."

For a second, she looked disbelieving, but she moved on. "Are you working already with a lender, by any chance? I can give you a list of excellent choices if you're not."

Outside the clear cubicle, a steady parade of people kept going past, most sneaking a look their way. "No need. It'll be a cash purchase."

She was obviously accustomed to hearing that particular answer. "That makes things very simple. Is there some area of Austin that particularly interests you?"

"No, ma'am." Grayson Gear had claimed its headquarters in Austin since the start, though most of his involvement was conducted from wherever he was on the road. He'd competed in plenty of rodeos in the area, though he knew only certain parts of town, and generally liked what he knew. "My personal knowledge of the city is limited, actually. I'm not from here."

Her gaze slid his way again. "Is your relocation for business purposes?"

"Mostly."

She looked back at her computer. "And where are you coming from?"

"All over." That was true enough. His actual home was Paseo, Texas. But few people had heard of the minuscule town, much less knew where it was. Ever since news had gotten out that Gerald Robinson aka Jerome Fortune was his and his triplet brothers' absentee biological father, though, the journalists and the Grayson groupies had been getting too damn close to ruining the peace there that he was determined to protect. His employees at Grayson Gear had been operating just fine for years despite his frequent absences, but they could always be counted on to keep interlopers away from his door when he *was* there. Especially Gerald Robinson, despite him being a fixture on the Austin landscape.

Grayson's lack of a precise answer didn't seem to bother Billie. Her finger continued sliding on the glass as the form on the screen slowly filled. "Then you haven't looked at any houses already?"

"Nope." He shifted and hitched one boot on top of his knee. They were brand-new Castletons, and as fine as the custom boots were, he preferred the ones he tramped around in at the ranch in Paseo where he and his brothers had grown up. They were Castletons, too. Bought nearly twenty years ago out of his first big win and just getting real comfortable now.

He and his Grayson Gear manager, Jessica Monroe, had been working on establishing a line of Castletons specifically for the company. But progress was slow. Castleton was an old family business and getting in the door was difficult. Considering his numerous endorsement deals, the challenge with Castleton had only made Grayson more determined. He'd even enlisted his mother's help. Though she'd been managing his rodeo career since the get-go, she generally left Grayson Gear business to him. Always said she had enough keeping her busy without adding that to her plate. But since she happened to think Castleton was the best bootmaker around, he'd talked her around to it.

"Haven't worked with any other Realtor?"

His eyes drifted past his boots to land on the curve of Billie's hip where she sat. The chair was black, making the white of her skirt seem even whiter. Below the hem, her smooth thighs were golden. "No, ma'am. You're my first."

He caught a wisp of blush rise in her cheeks and saw

her moisten her lips again. He couldn't help smiling a little. Women often blushed around him, but none quite as charmingly as she.

Blushing or not, she stayed on course. "You're probably anxious to get on with properties to view, so we can finish up the rest of the details along the way." She tapped her glass-driven mouse and tiny images filled the screen. "Why don't you tell me what you're looking for? You want your forever home? Or something more short-term?"

Until Gerald Robinson came calling, he'd considered Paseo to be his home. "Forever."

Her smile deepened, as if his answer pleased her. "What kind of home? Single family? Condo? Any particular square footage in mind? Number of bedrooms? Lot size?"

"No condos. Only bedroom I care about is mine." But logic made him consider. He'd need more bedrooms if his brothers came to visit. Jayden and Ariana didn't have kids yet, but considering they couldn't keep their hands off each other, it was only a matter of time before they did. And Nathan and Bianca already had her little boy, EJ. Then there was his mom. He'd need a room for her, or even a guest house that she could call her own. One appealing enough to keep her safely away from Robinson.

"I guess six bedrooms ought to do. A guest house would be a plus." He banished Gerald Robinson from his thoughts. He was enjoying Billie's company too much to ruin it thinking about the bastard.

"Any deal breakers? Something that would rule out a property right from the start?"

"No property. I need acreage for my horses and stock. I can always build my own barn, but I'll need the land first."

"Would you consider undeveloped land? Build your own house, too?"

"I'm hoping for something that won't take that long. I'd like this wrapped up before summer's done."

She nodded. "Any particular features in the house that you require?"

"Like what?" He saw the same ripe blonde who'd already passed Billie's office several times make yet another round. Bolder than most, she gave him a direct smile and pressed her hands together over her heart. He automatically grinned a response and she stopped dead in her tracks. At least until an older man with a frown passed her, and she scurried away.

"If you prefer single-story, or must have a wine cellar, fireplace, pool," Billie was saying. "Things like that."

"I'm more beer than wine." He shrugged. "No particular preference. Just want a place I can put away the bedroll."

Her eyebrows lifted. "Bedroll?"

"Figure of speech," he said dismissively. Though it wasn't. He still traveled between rodeos with a bedroll in his truck. He could afford hotels now, but sometimes it was easier to bed down with the horses in the trailer, or under the stars. "I'm on the road a lot. Just need a place to land. And not too close to the city." He would never be able to replicate the ranch in Paseo, but he could try. "I like my space and my privacy. As for the house, I guess a fireplace for cold days. AC on hot." He grinned. "Running water and electricity."

Her smile edged toward impish again. "I've always thought they were convenient."

"'Course, that's when the fireplace comes in handy... good place to keep warm. 'Specially with the right company."

Her cheeks pinkened again. "And your budget?"

Did he have one? He supposed he should. He kept his eye on the broad levels, but Deborah kept her finger on all of the finer points. He knew he could walk away from rodeoing tomorrow and all of his resulting endorsements without personally missing the money a speck. Grayson Gear had become far more profitable in the last decade than anything else he did. But he had rodeoing in his blood. It kept Grayson Gear's name prominent, and as a result, he was able to keep his charitable efforts funded.

Which meant as long as he was physically able to rodeo, he would. Even if the rest of the rodeo world was starting to consider him ancient.

Billie was still looking at him inquiringly. Her hair had slipped free of her enticing ear and she tucked it there once more as she waited.

He felt thirsty all over again.

He tapped the toe of his boot. "Darlin', when I find the right one, no price'll be too high."

Her eyes did flicker at that. Still the model of decorum, though, she looked back at her screen and glided her fingers on her glass pad again.

"Does it get to you, working in a fishbowl like this?" He gestured at the clear, short walls, and the middle-aged redhead who'd been passing Billie's office with the speed of a snail suddenly picked up her pace.

Billie looked wry. "Everything here takes some getting used to. Particularly knowing the boss is always watching. He has a very strict code of ethics that I guess he wants to ensure we're all following."

"What does he expect to catch y'all doing? Stealing cucumbers and water?"

She smiled. "One of these days, I'm sure I won't even

notice all this glass at all. But it is very disconcerting when you first experience it."

"No kidding." His working life was fishbowl-ish, too, though it sure hadn't started out that way. Like a lot of the guys and gals competing in rodeo day in and day out, he'd done so in obscurity until a championship buckle was on his belt, and suddenly he had endorsement offers landing at his feet. "Probably not easy to get used to."

"No, but it's like what you've done in rodeo. You have a job to do and you get on with it."

His toe stopped tapping. "You *do* know who I am."

"It's hard *not* to know who you are. You've been on the news a few times this week. And then there are the Grayson Gear billboards around town." She smiled slightly. "Despite the impression of our local lookey-loos, you're not the first celebrity who's chosen to work with Austin Elite. All I care about is finding a perfect property for you, Mr. Smith." She waited a beat. "But if you prefer a more experienced agent—perhaps Elena. She's the blonde who has traipsed by a dozen times and she'd be entirely—"

"God, no. You, uh, you just surprised me for a bit." Bemused him, more like. "And it's not really Smith. It's Fortune."

She looked only mildly curious and he almost wished he hadn't said anything. Grayson Smith was simply the name he used on his professional bio. But at least his real last name hadn't raised any obvious flags for her.

Considering the way the Fortune name had been in the news since the revelation that Austin icon and bazillionaire Gerald Robinson was actually Jerome Fortune—an heir to even more millions who'd supposedly died a lifetime ago—it was a relief.

It was time to leave the subject of his name well

enough alone. "Mind if I pull my chair a little closer so I can see better?"

"Please do." She rolled her own chair a few inches over so he could edge nearer to the desk.

Nearer to her.

"I apologize again for the close quarters. I'm still the smallest fish in the pond here, so I don't get the pick of offices just yet. Or the pick of clients, so I have to thank you again for requesting me specifically, Mr. Fortune."

His mother had requested Billie, but who was he to correct her now?

"Just Grayson," he replied. He hadn't set out to be known only by his given name any more than he'd set out to be a celebrity. Over the years, it had sort of cemented itself in the public eye. But ever since his mother had admitted that she hadn't simply decided to use the last name Fortune because of her good fortune when she gave birth to healthy triplets, but had actually given them their *father's* name, he'd been increasingly happy not to use it.

Which was a line of thinking certain to put him in a bad mood.

And Billie—young or not—was too much of an unexpected pleasure for him to be in a bad mood thinking about the bastard who'd sired him and his brothers.

He maneuvered his chair almost next to her. It meant he had to stretch one leg out her office door, where someone might trip over it as they dawdled and gawked, but he didn't much care. "And I'm not complaining about the tight space." He nodded toward her computer screen. "All right, darlin'. Show me what you've got."

Chapter Two

Thirty minutes later, Billie watched Grayson stride out the Austin Elite front door. She held her breath and turned to face the receptionist.

Amberleigh Gardner was fanning herself. "That man makes even an old woman like me feel faint. And you're the lucky girl who gets to work with him." She winked. "You know he's not married."

Hoping that she was hiding the shakiness she'd felt since realizing that her prospective client Mr. Smith was *The* Grayson—famous rodeo rider, local business owner, endorser of everything from beer to saddles—Billie calmly started back to her office. "He's a client, Amberleigh. No more or less important than any other client. His marital status isn't relevant."

Right.

Which was why she'd darn near tripped over her own feet in shock when she'd come out to greet her new client and recognized him. "Besides, you know the rules." No romantic involvement with clients. It was DeForest Allen's sacrosanct rule after having seen too many deals go south because of it.

"Keep tellin' yourself that, hon. Some girls would think losing a job over a guy like *that* to be well worth it." Amberleigh smiled knowingly as Billie passed her.

Once in the office that she'd been assigned three weeks ago when she began working with Austin Elite, she moved the chair Grayson had used back to its usual position before sitting down in her own chair.

Then it felt like all the strength in her body left her and she dropped her head onto her desk. Not caring if anyone *did* see.

From the top of his wavy, caramel-brown hair to the bottom of his expensive boots, Grayson was six-plus feet of drop-dead gorgeous.

Her skin felt flushed and her heart was racing.

She definitely needed to get herself under control before she met him the next day.

"How'd it go with the reigning King of Rodeo, Belinda?"

She sat bolt upright, assuming a confident smile for her boss. She didn't believe for one second that DeForest Allen had known *who* her prospective client was before Grayson arrived, any more than Billie had. "It went very well, Mr. Allen. I'm setting up a tour of six properties for tomorrow morning."

He nodded his silver head. "Close the deal quickly, Belinda. We don't want another Dickinson situation."

"No, we don't, sir." But inwardly, she'd tensed. She'd hoped by moving from Houston and back home to Austin, she'd have left the Dickinson situation behind her. She reminded herself that she'd been here only a few weeks, though. And trust took time.

Plus the proof of signed sales contracts. Dickinson aside, Billie had had plenty of those since getting her license years earlier. Reminding her boss of them, though, was probably not very politic. Despite her track record, she was still surprised he'd hired her. Austin Elite was the premiere agency in town. She'd never actually expected to be offered a position there.

He cupped the steel door frame of her cubicle, oblivious to the clear fingerprints he left on the glass. He was the firm's owner and broker, so they were his glass walls to smear up however he wanted. "Don't wait for the weekly status meeting to keep me posted."

"I won't," she promised.

She waited until he'd entered his own office before letting out another breath.

Did he think *she* wanted another Dickinson situation? Rhonda Dickinson, reeking of Texas oil money, had been a nightmare of a client, pulling out at the last minute on three different sales because she'd happened to find something that looked "just a teensy bit better" each time.

Of course, they hadn't been better in the end, either.

Ultimately, she'd blamed Billie—and subsequently the Houston-based agency she'd worked for—for her own inability to commit, and took her business to their chief competitor.

Last Billie had heard, Rhonda still hadn't signed her name on the bottom of a purchase contract. It was some small comfort, she supposed. If Billie would have been able to get the woman to commit, it would have been her largest sale to date. But now Billie had Grayson Smith—make that Grayson *Fortune*—as a client.

The Fortune name was a big one around Texas. She couldn't help but wonder if he was connected to it.

Her phone chimed musically and she automatically reached out to answer it. "Billie Pemberton."

"You goin' to Selena's birthday party this week?"

At the sound of her cousin Max's voice, Billie glanced at the photos sitting on top of her filing cabinet and plucked one from the collection, of Max taking down a steer. She'd used the excuse of putting Grayson's water glass there earlier to turn the shot of her cousin away from her new client's view. "I'm bringing the cupcakes and Mom's hosting, so yes. You?" Selena was the daughter of a mutual cousin.

Max laughed. "You know I'd skip it if my ma wouldn't make my life miserable for it. Too bad I'm not on the road somewhere."

"When are you heading out again?" Even though they each had four older siblings of their own, she and Max had been close as thieves their entire lives. Didn't hurt that their mothers were sisters, so they'd been raised more like brother and sister than cousins. Now, when Max wasn't out at some rodeo, he stayed with his folks, Mae and Larry. Billie had a one-bedroom apartment in downtown Austin, into which she was still moving her stuff from Houston.

She opened the bottom drawer of the cabinet and tucked the picture of Max inside. She'd leave it there, where there would be no chance of her newest client spotting it.

It was pretty unlikely the rodeo star would care that she had a photo of the young man who'd bested him in El Paso, but she wasn't going to take chances.

Nor was she going to take chances that Max would learn the identity of her new high-profile client. After what had happened earlier that year, he'd consider it treason.

"Coleman starts the day after Selena's deal, so we'll

drive over once it looks like I can git along without Mama getting ticked."

"Travis going?" When Max's buddy Travis Conrad wasn't competing in tie-down roping, he hazed for Max.

"Yeah. Hopefully, we'll still have enough time to catch some z's before slack."

"Slack," she knew, was the time scheduled for over-flow contestants to compete, because they couldn't all be scheduled into the regular nightly performances. It was generally free to get into, whereas the performances were not. Fortunately for the competitors, a slack event counted just as much as a performance event. Like Max said, the paycheck was the same whether there were paying crowds in the grandstand or not.

Of course, a lot of times that paycheck was a big fat zero. Considering the entrance fees, as well as the cost of getting themselves, their gear and their horse, if they even had one there in the first place, rodeoing often meant cowboys headed on down the road already in the hole. Max loved it, though.

Personally, Billie liked having a bank account that wasn't always in need of life support.

She turned back to face her desk. "And after Coleman?" She tapped her glass keyboard, systematically printing off the listings Grayson had liked, as well as a few more to recommend if needed.

The Fourth of July was less than a month away and she knew Max would be particularly busy. "How many rodeos are you packing in this year?"

The few weeks in and around the Independence Day holiday were affectionately known as Cowboy Christmas because of the sheer number of opportunities a person had to enter the most rodeos for the most money.

"Long as my truck, trailer and gear hold out, seven,

including Reno. Got three saddle bronc riders plus Trav hitching rides with me. Helps a lot on expenses and the driving when we'll be covering some four thousand miles."

She grimaced, just thinking about five men packed into such close confines. She remembered one year after he'd returned from Cowboy Christmas. Ripe didn't even begin to describe the state of his truck. She wondered if Grayson would be caught up in the frenzied schedule, too. If he were, it would definitely put a crimp in his availability to see listings. "Going to Calgary?"

"The earnings don't count toward the standings. Cowboy Country's will. So that's where I'm planning to be. You gonna make it over for the rodeo?"

Her fingers paused on the glass. Cowboy Country USA was a popular Western-theme amusement park in Horseback Hollow, where their mothers had grown up. It was a good five to six hour drive. "Depends on work."

Max made a sound. "Everything depends on your work. You're gonna get old and dull, Bill. You need to get out and have more fun. And by fun, I mean sex."

Her fingers paused. "And the last time *you* had some fun?"

He snorted, laughing. "About a week ago. A chick I met at Twine."

"Obviously, you're not still brokenhearted from Bethany." Bethany Belmont was the barrel racer Grayson supposedly stole from Max back in March. Max claimed Bethany had been the love of his life until Grayson lured her away. It was then that Max had made it his goal to unseat the reigning rodeo champion.

"Being brokenhearted ain't got diddly to do with sex." Max's voice had gone flat.

She rolled her eyes and started typing again. If Grayson were still involved with the woman, he'd given no indication of it that morning. And she found it difficult to believe that her cousin had been as gung ho over the barrel racer as he claimed, since Max fell in love more often than Billie bought shoes. "I can't believe that of the two of us, *you* are the romantic."

"Yeah, well, you ought t' try it sometime. At least go out and drink a little. Dance a little. Never know where it might lead."

"Yeah, well, you know how I feel about that," she returned calmly. It wasn't that she didn't believe in love. Her parents had been inseparable since being childhood sweethearts. Billie just wasn't willing to sacrifice everything she wanted out of life because of it. She wanted her high-rise apartment that she could barely afford. She wanted her nice clothes and her interesting career and—one day—a bank account that allowed for more things than just the minimum daily requirements. So far, any relationships she'd had of the romantic variety had been decided letdowns in comparison.

"Look, Max, I've got stuff to do. Don't forget to bring Selena an appropriate gift. A bottle of hooch for a thirteen-year-old won't cut it."

"You give me no credit. Last time I did that was for Audie's eighteenth."

"Eighteen was still underage, Max," she reminded him before hanging up and turning her attention fully to the property listings once more.

When she met with Grayson in the morning, she wanted to be completely prepared. She'd been told to close the deal quickly, and that's exactly what she intended to do.

When the phone rang a few seconds later, she grabbed

it up again. "If you're calling to ask me to buy Selena's gift for you, the answer is still no."

A feminine laugh answered her. "Actually, I was calling to see if you were going to be in Houston this Friday."

Billie's fingers relaxed on her glass keypad again. "Well, if it isn't the soon-to-be Mrs. Zach McCarter." She grinned. "Or after enduring Schuyler's wedding last month, are you calling to tell me you and Zach decided to forgo all the hoopla and elope to Vegas?"

Maddie Fortunado laughed in her ear again. "We're still planning a wedding," she assured her. "So don't think you're getting out of attending. But I guarantee it won't be quite as over-the-top as my sister's come-one, come-all grand affair. So, are you going to be in Houston on Friday? We're trying out a new restaurant and I wanted to let you know in case you're able to join the gang."

Maddie was the newly crowned president at Fortunado Real Estate in Houston along with her fiancé, Zach, where Billie had gotten her start. She'd also been the one to invite her to join the "gang"—a group of young real estate professionals who met routinely to talk business and socialize.

"I hope to be," Billie told her. "I've still got a couple loads of stuff to move from my old apartment."

"Some people would just hire a moving company," Maddie pointed out.

Some people didn't have the extra money to do that. Billie kept the fact to herself. "I'm still helping the Montanegros navigate their home purchase in Houston," she said, which was true. "So I still have to be there occasionally, anyway."

"Oh, right. Your old neighbors. The ones you're forgoing your sales commission for."

"The ones who are storing my stuff in their garage,"

Billie added humorously. "It's the least I could do. So where's the meeting place?" She made a note when Maddie told her.

"How is business going at Austin Elite? Any new listings?"

It was all too easy to conjure Grayson's face in her mind. "No new listings. But a new client looking to buy came in today specifically asking for me."

"That's great, Billie! I knew it wouldn't be long before you were right back in the swing of things. Word gets around when you're a good agent. So what size fishy cracker are we talking?"

Billie chuckled. "He's a big one, if I haven't just jinxed everything by admitting it."

"He?" Maddie's voice piqued with interest. "Is he single?"

"Maddie! I don't know who is worse—my cousin with sex on his brain, or you with romance on yours."

"May I just say that those two elements *can* work quite well together? I'll take your nonanswer as the affirmative, though. So is the male big fish *eligible*? Do tell."

She could imagine Maddie's reaction if she knew just how eligible. "There's nothing to tell!" Particularly when DeForest Allen walked past her office again, giving her a close look. "I'll tell you as much as I can on Friday if I can make it. Right now, my boss is giving me the stink eye. And I've told you what he's like."

"That's what you get for defecting back to Austin," Maddie said humorously. "Fine. But I'm holding you to it, my friend. So be prepared with details the next time I see you!"

Grayson slid the key card over the lock on his hotel suite on the top floor of the Kimpton and pushed open the door. His mother, seated on a couch positioned to take in the lake view, looked up at him. She had her usual calendar spread in front of her, along with her phone and a foot-high stack of glossy Grayson publicity stills that she was signing.

"How'd it go?"

He dropped his hat on the table next to the stack. "Did you know that Billy with a *y* is actually Billie with an *i* and an *e*?"

"Don't let your sexism show, son." The fact that Deborah followed his statement at all was proof enough that she had known. She signed another photo with a flourish. "I can't help what you assumed."

"Then did you know how *young* she is?"

Deborah leaned back against the couch. As usual, her long brown hair hung over her shoulder in a thick braid, and she had another pen tucked behind her ear, almost hiding the few sprinkles of gray she possessed. "Everything I've heard about Billie Pemberton when she was in Houston is that she is an excellent agent. Astute. Hardworking, and most importantly—according to *your* specifications—*very* discreet. Why would you care whether she's twenty-one or ninety-one?" The fine lines at the corners of her eyes crinkled. "Or was she attractive, too?"

There was a price to be paid for having his mother act as his manager. When most men were off on their own, catching grief for not calling home often enough, Deborah Fortune handled almost every detail in Grayson's life. With finesse and grace when necessary, but more often than not with plain speaking and a no-bull attitude. It's how she'd raised him and his brothers when they were kids, and it was how things were now.

"Yeah, she was attractive." He sounded grouchy and

didn't care. He flung himself down on the other couch and started to stretch out his legs.

"Don't get comfortable. You need to sign some of these, too." She pushed a stack of stills toward him. She waited until he'd sat forward and grabbed a pen. "So you liked her."

After so many years traveling on the road together, they usually both knew how to give each other privacy and space. Evidently, this was not going to be one of those times.

He slid his gaze across the table toward her as he signed his name. Autographing the photographs they gave away during his appearances had gotten so mundane, he could do it in his sleep. "Like you said. She seems competent so far." And beautiful. Intelligent.

And sexy as all hell, the way the bridge of her nose wrinkled when she really concentrated.

He turned back to the stack of photos, but the image in his head was all Billie. "I'm meeting her tomorrow morning to look at a couple properties."

"Tomorrow." Deborah sounded surprised. "That's nice, but that's not what I was asking."

How well he knew it. "I'm looking for a new ranch, Ma. Not a wife."

Deborah clucked her tongue. "Don't be so reactionary. I'm not suggesting you get married tomorrow. I'm merely suggesting you don't have many opportunities to meet nice young women, and when you do, you should pay attention."

"I meet nice young women all the time. I don't need to be dating my real estate agent."

"So you've already thought about it."

His glare at her had no effect. So he gave up and

grabbed more photos from the stack. "How many of these did we print?"

"Five thousand. And usually, the women you meet are reporters and sales reps and buckle bunnies."

"Ariana's a reporter." Or a novelist. He wasn't exactly sure what Jayden's new wife was working on at the moment. "She wasn't a nice young woman?"

Deborah sighed noisily. "You know I already love Ariana and Bianca like daughters. And don't get me started on how EJ's already wrapping his hands around my heart."

"He *is* a cute little dickens." Grayson's brother Nathan would be a heck of a stepfather for the four-year-old now that he'd married Bianca. "I took out that rep from Change Sportswear I met a couple weeks ago. Dinner at a place with tablecloths and everything." Followed by a very entertaining evening in her bed. Like him, Livian Reed wanted nothing more out of their very brief acquaintance than that.

Good food. Good sex. Goodbye.

Just the way he liked it. No promises, no strings.

Too-young-for-him Billie Pemberton might be perfect in every way. But she wasn't a no-strings type. He hadn't even needed to see all the family photographs crammed on her filing cabinet to know it.

"Livian Reed's a buckle bunny, too. She's just dressed in Ann Taylor."

He couldn't help but grin. "And Livian would eviscerate you for the comparison if she ever knew."

His mother's expression turned dry. "Well, you're not going to see her again, I know that for certain, so I'm not going to lose sleep worrying that she'll find out."

"I oughta call Livian and take her out again just to make you sweat a little."

"Two dates with the same girl? The last time *that* happened, you were eighteen and hot after Bethany Belmont." Deborah laughed knowingly and pushed off the couch. "You've got me shaking in my Castletons, kiddo."

"Speaking of." He was glad to change the subject. "Any progress on that front?"

She opened the suite's minibar and studied the contents. "I'm still waiting for a call back from them. I'm not sure how much I can do, son, if the lure of The Grayson hasn't already impressed them."

He grunted. "Thanks."

"Want me to start pandering to your ego now? If this is a midlife crisis starting, just tell me now." She pulled out a bottle of fruit juice and eyed him with amusement as she shook it. "I'll head on back to Paseo most happily and leave you to your buckle bunnies, who will coo and awe your ego right up to its fullest—"

"Yeah, yeah," he said, cutting her off. She'd head back to Paseo and the ranch. Gerald Robinson might find out—God knew the tech giant had means that seemed to defy all imagination—and come sniffing around her and…no thank you, ma'am. From what Jayden had told Grayson about his last encounter with Gerald, there'd been real emotion on the man's face when he'd spoken of Deborah. Didn't matter that the man—whatever the hell name he was using—was married. Robinson's infidelities were the world's worst-kept secret. Grayson didn't believe for a second that their life would have been different if Gerald had known Deborah gave birth to his three sons. And Grayson intended to do whatever he needed to do to keep the man from ever hurting his mom again.

Fortunately unaware of his dark thoughts, his mother deepened her smile. "You know I'll always help you if you ask. But one of these days, son, you won't need me along to manage your rodeo career. Or you won't want me along. Or you'll realize it's finally time to give your body a break and retire from bulldogging. Neither one of us could have guessed how your teenage hobby would change our lives. But it can't last forever. And that's okay. Life moves on. As it should."

"I'm not retiring until I've got one more world championship to my name." The National Finals Rodeo would be held in Las Vegas in December. He was already tied for the most world championship wins ever. One more would set a new record. And *then* he'd retire from bulldogging.

Ego? Yeah. He knew he had more than his fair share of ego. But it was also calculated. Record-winning names faded from memory a little more slowly than also-rans. And the longer he could make money on his name, the longer he could put that money to good use.

"Well, I for one am glad you're already number three in the money," his mother said. "Between rodeoing, Grayson Gear and your charity appearances, you've worked nearly every day for the past year. One of these days, it's going to take its toll on you."

He wasn't worried about the toll. Aches and pains went hand in hand with rodeoing. "I'd be second in the standings if I hadn't bought it in Silver City and lost out to Max Vargas."

The entire season of pro rodeo was about the money rankings. Earnings were the only common ground on which to judge their success as they competed in rodeos throughout the country under every condition that could be had. If the Finals were the goal—and admittedly, for the majority of cowboys who competed it was not—then nearly every dollar earned paved the way there.

"Vargas can really run a steer," his mother pointed out mildly.

"And at the rate he's going, he'll be at the Nationals. But he's still a punk and I don't like losing to a punk."

Deborah looked amused. "There was a day when Joe-Don Gainer called you a punk."

"Yeah, and Joe-Don was right then. Same as I'm right, now. I'm not the saint that Joe-Don was, though. Hazing for me like he did even though he was a Hall of Famer?" Grayson shook his head. "Won't catch me hazing for Max Vargas. If his usual guy, Travis, isn't hazing for him, he treats the one who is like dirt."

A wrestler who didn't appreciate the contribution of his hazer—who rode on the opposite side of the steer, keeping him more or less straight and close to the bulldogger—was just damn stupid. Luck of the draw chose the steer. The hazer and the wrestler's skill together determined what they did with that luck.

"Don't go off on a tangent dissecting details of Silver City again," his mother warned. "The hour you subjected me to the other day was enough." She finally opened her juice and wandered to look out the windows. "I wonder if I should just show up at Castleton's doorway. Might be harder for them to ignore me in person. Red Rock's only a couple hours from here. I could rent a car and drive over and be back before we need to leave for Coleman. What do you think?"

"I think once the event tomorrow is finished, you could go to Red Rock, and from there head straight to Coleman." He gave her a look. "I can manage to get myself and the trailer and the horses there without you."

"I realize you're capable." Her tone turned dry again. "Whether you manage to do it all in time to not miss your event altogether is the question."

"Last time I did that was fifteen years ago."

"Because of a girl—"

"And I haven't been late once since," he said, cutting her off. "Even though you still harp on it often enough. Focus on Red Rock and let me worry about getting to Coleman." He lifted his pen. "We don't need five thousand of these things for tomorrow, do we?" The remaining unsigned stack was still a foot high.

"I think they're hoping for about a thousand to show."

He capped the pen and tossed it on the cocktail table, stretching his fingers. "What time's the deal supposed to start?"

"Two o'clock. I've personally taped up copies of your schedule this week in this suite. I told you that you didn't have to make the appearance tomorrow. If you hadn't, you would have had time with Billie to see more." She smiled knowingly. "More than just a couple properties, I mean."

He let that pass.

The library appearance had been added to his already busy schedule there in Austin at the last minute, and his personal appearance fee would go to local literacy. "It's a good cause." He hadn't taken the military route that Nathan and Jayden had. They'd been literally out saving the world. Instead, all Grayson could offer was his name and his money to support charitable efforts where he could. And he knew Deborah understood his motivations completely.

"I'll be finished with Billie in plenty of time to meet you here before the dedication." He pushed to his feet and stretched. "I'm going to hit the gym this afternoon and then see if I can scare up a massage somewhere."

His mom rolled her eyes. "Read your schedule!" She headed toward the connecting door that separated Grayson's suite from her own. "I've arranged a massage for you right here at four o'clock. Don't forget to tip your masseuse and don't forget to meet me at seven. We're having drinks with the Deckers at Twine."

He groaned. Claudia and Myron Decker had more money than Midas and could always be counted on to support his foundation, Grayson Good. But in the process, they definitely liked to trot him out as if he were their prized bull. Ergo the appearance the next day at the new library. "It's never just drinks with the Deckers."

"And whose fault is that?" She gave him one more pointed look. "They're bankrolling the event tomorrow, so wear a clean shirt and don't be late."

Chapter Three

Billie was wearing another short skirt complete with the intriguing zipper running right up over her backside.

Only difference today was that her skirt was black and the silky tank top that exposed her tanned shoulders was white. The high-heeled shoes were red, and the legs they showed off were still flat-out stunning.

She had her hair pulled back into a thick ponytail at the back of her head. The hairstyle not only exposed the trio of earrings on the upper curve of her ear, but the long, long line of her throat.

"Talk about perfect timing," she called to him as he jaywalked across the street toward the real estate office. She gestured at the dark gray luxury sedan parked at the curb next to her. "I just got here, myself." She waited until he reached her side of the street. "Where did you park?"

"I walked from my hotel."

Her bright smile turned stricken as she scurried to the

passenger door and opened it. "I'm so sorry. I should have offered to pick you up. It didn't even occur to me to—"

"No apologies, darlin'," he interrupted, looking at her over the top rims of his sunglasses. "I liked the walk." It was a good way to work out his muscle kinks and some of his hangover from the night before. "And it gave me a chance to get this." He lifted his oversize takeout coffee.

Her smile widened once more. She reached inside the vehicle, giving him an eye-popping view of her inner knee and thigh. Then she straightened and he belatedly noticed the identical cup she'd retrieved.

"If you tell me that's straight-up black coffee, I may have to marry you right now."

Her cheeks turned red, but she laughed. "Fortunately, all the hopeful women of the world can rest easy this morning. It's iced chai tea."

He made a face. "That's almost as bad as cucumber-laced water."

She laughed again and stepped out of the way. "Maybe I can redeem myself by offering plenty of legroom. Your chariot, Mr. Fortune."

"Told you. Just Grayson." He ducked his head and climbed into the passenger seat of the spacious car.

It was the kind of vehicle a wealthy grandmother might drive. Definitely not what he'd expect of a young woman like Billie.

He waited until she'd climbed behind the wheel and strapped herself in with the seat belt. "Company car?"

She laughed yet again, but wryly this time. "Don't I wish. I'd much prefer the payment to be on Austin Elite's bank account than on mine. But no." She patted the leather-wrapped steering wheel. "She's all mine. Or will be after six more payments to the bank. It's not the newest model, but it's comfortable and gets me where my clients and I need to go."

"Sort of how I feel about my truck." He'd had many over the years, but could easily remember when his truck had been his largest investment. "Not the newest but it gets me where my horses and I need to go."

"Wasn't a new truck one of the prizes last year at the Cowboy Country rodeo?"

Surprised, he gave her a look. Rather than settle her cup of nasty-ass tea next to his coffee in the console, she'd tucked it between her knees and was starting the engine. He *had* won the new truck, but had turned around and auctioned it off through Grayson Good for a children's charity. "You actually follow rodeo?"

"I come from a large family," she said. "They're into everything from baseball to zebra racing." Her cheeks still looked a little red as she pulled on a pair of gold-rimmed aviator sunglasses and checked the traffic before zipping out into it.

Given the sudden speed, he was glad he'd already fastened his seat belt. And also glad they were essentially driving around in a small tank.

"So…" She reached behind her seat and retrieved a fancy folder that she handed to him. "I've printed all the listings we reviewed yesterday, plus a few more that I think might be of interest, too. There's also a map if you're inclined to follow along." She nipped the big car between two semitrucks with about six inches to spare.

He grabbed his cup and wished there was something stronger inside it than just French roast.

She raced through a light more yellow than green, braked slightly around a curve and sped up a freeway on-ramp. "Is it too windy for you?" His window was halfway down and hers was all the way down, making her long ponytail fly around her head.

"Wind's good." Aside from the fact that she looked young and beautiful and vibrant, he was hoping he wouldn't have to hang his head out the window.

It wasn't that he was uncomfortable with her fast—make that maniacal, he decided when she shot across two lanes of traffic—driving.

It was more the combination of her obvious lead foot and the evening-into-night of drinks with the Deckers the night before. Then everything had gotten out of control, and the cops had been called, and a news crew showed up...

He planted his ball cap more firmly on his head and sucked on the coffee. He'd warned his mom that drinks with the Deckers was never a simple thing. Even when they were trying to do something good like sponsor the library deal. "Which place are we heading to first?"

Billie held the steering wheel and her tea in one hand and reached over to the folder she'd dropped on his lap, and he damn near choked on his coffee. But all she did was flip open the folder to reveal a colorful printed map.

"Property number one." She lightly tapped the page, then returned her hand to the steering wheel. Evidently, only to maneuver the car right back across the same two lanes of traffic.

He closed his eyes. Give him six hundred pounds of ornery steer any day.

"The properties are numbered in the order we'll see them," she said above the wind. "I know it's easy for the properties to blur together, which is why I've prepared the folio. You can make notes as you like."

She reached behind her seat again and produced a slender gold pen tastefully monogrammed with "Austin Elite" on the side. She handed it to him. "Three of the properties this morning are vacant, including this first one. I find my clients usually prefer visiting vacant properties. Makes it easier to imagine living there." She zipped around another semitruck. "Weather is supposed to be hotter than usual today. I have several bottles of chilled water if—"

He lifted his hand just in case she intended to reach behind her seat again. "I'm good for now. Thanks."

She sent him another smile. "Great. I love a morning drive." She changed lanes again. "Just gets the blood flowing, you know?"

He managed a smile. The only thing getting his blood flowing that morning was the vivid smile on her pretty face. That, and the knowledge that his life insurance was up-to-date.

Fortunately, the farther outside of town they traveled, the thinner the traffic grew. Then, at least, he didn't worry so much about colliding with other vehicles as much as flying off the highway curves. After about thirty minutes more, she pulled off the freeway and began working her way through the mercifully empty countryside to the first property.

Even though this whole thing was his idea, it still felt strange when she pulled to a stop in front of the first house.

"Here we are at last."

It was a brick two-story with two wings and not another house in sight. But imagining himself living there was beyond him.

"The property is on city water." She pushed her glasses up onto her head before gathering up the Magic Bag hiding behind her seat, then climbed out of the car. "As you can see from the printout, there is a little over five acres." She looked down at the ground beneath them, waving one arm. "The entire drive is covered in pavers—antique terra-cotta color, I believe. Very attractive." She looked up at him over the top of the car and he gave what he hoped was a suitable response.

Her sales litany didn't lose any steam, so he supposed it must have sufficed.

"The iron entrance gate was left open now for us, but it's electronically controlled. So you wouldn't have to worry about any Grayson groupies coming out to bother you."

He gave her a quick look. He hadn't used that particular term with her. "I don't have groupies." It was blatantly untrue, even though he wished otherwise.

"Sorry." She looked contrite. "I saw the news this morning about what happened at Twine last night. The term was just in my head."

He sighed. "Overeager fans who'd had way too much to drink. Unfortunately, it happens occasionally." Particularly when he was out in public with people like the Deckers, who felt compelled to make a big deal about their "celebrity" friend.

"Did that one woman actually punch the news cameraman?"

He grimaced. Two women from the bar, bolstered by booze and who knew what else, had been intent on joining their party. "Only after he told her he wasn't putting her on camera unless she put her shirt back on. It pretty much turned into a free-for-all after that."

"Did you really pay her jail fine?"

"It seemed the right thing to do at the time." He stared at the house. "Maybe an electronic gate would be a good thing, after all."

"Or maybe avoid places like Twine," she said humorously.

He grunted. "Ever been there?"

"A time or twenty. It's the best place for martinis and tapas." She gestured toward the house. "Would you like to see inside?"

He shrugged and closed the car door. "That's what we're here for."

She gave him a winning smile again. "Don't forget your folio if you want to make notes."

He reached back in for the fancy folder of information she'd prepared, and followed her toward the front door of the house.

"I haven't been here before, but I know it's on a lockbox." Her high heels clicked on the paver stones as she searched for the box holding the house key. "In addition to the three garages off to your left, there's a structure in the rear of the house that could also be used as a garage or for some other type of storage. Ah. There it is." She knelt down behind a tastefully positioned bush, and straightened a moment later, doing a little shimmy to push the hem of her narrow skirt back down toward her knees. She glanced his way as she unlocked the enormous front door. "The position on this hill gives a nice view. And I've heard that the adjacent land may be available for the right price. It's totally undeveloped and would mean an additional ten acres. Have any initial thoughts?"

The nice view he was looking at had more to do with her than the location of the house. Which wasn't exciting him in the least. The vegetation dotting the hillside was more cactus and scrub than grassland. "Let's just see what we've got inside."

She swept open the door and waited for him to enter.

He walked inside. The house might be vacant of occupants, but it wasn't vacant of furnishings. Beneath the vaulted entry, an ornate neon-green chandelier hung over a bright purple statue of a rearing horse.

For a minute, he wished he was back home in Paseo, where the only times you used the front entrance of the house—versus the back door—was if company was coming over for Christmas dinner. Where everyone in town knew who he was and didn't give two figs about his supposed "celebrity" status. And where anyone with two licks of common sense knew better than to hang a butt-ugly green chandelier over an even uglier purple horse.

"That's a bold design choice," Billie said faintly.

"It's ugly as hell," he said bluntly. "And I like horses."

"Just keep in mind that the furnishings aren't permanent fixtures. They'll all be leaving along with the owners. Do you want to see more, or shall we move on?"

Despite the hideous horse, the high ceilings and the view outside, the inside of the house felt like a cave to him. "Move on, if you don't mind."

"Of course not. You're the buyer, after all. Walking in the door should feel like home to you." She juggled the materials in her arm and came up with a business card. "I just need to leave my card. I'll meet you at the car."

He gave the hideous statue a wide berth and went back outside. He thought again about the ranch in Paseo. There, the house wasn't even a third of the size of this one, but it was surrounded by a whole lot more prime grazing land. Would he ever find a place that felt like home when he walked in the door, besides the house in which he'd grown up?

He headed back to the car and his now-cool coffee. He drank it anyway.

Within minutes, Billie had locked up the house again and they were off to property number two.

It excited him no more than property number one.

The land was decent enough, though still too little of it. There were two barns, and five bedrooms in the house.

Knowing that he'd given short shrift to property number one, this time he forced himself to traipse through every room of the streamlined home.

"No?" Billie gave him a questioning look as he paused in the state-of-the-art kitchen. It was all stainless steel, which he didn't mind here, but it matched the stainless steel and glass that dominated the rest of the house, too. Which he did mind.

Frankly, the place had the antiseptic air of a hospital. And having spent his entire adult life wrestling with horned beasts, he'd had more than his share of hospitals.

"Afraid not." He remembered his mom's admonishments to be polite when he'd set out that morning. "Sorry."

Billie waved away Grayson's apology. Seeing two houses without a spark of excitement wasn't anything to get worried about.

Yet.

"Don't be sorry," she told him. "Each time we see something, it helps me narrow down what you're really looking for." At least that was her theory.

She stepped around him to leave her card among the collection already sitting on the steel counter and led the way back out of the austere house.

Unlike the day before, when he'd walked through the door of the real estate office looking like the poster boy for professional rodeo, today Grayson wore slouchy beige cargo shorts, leather flip-flops and a Dallas Cowboys ball cap. The calves showing below the long shorts were just as tanned and muscular as the arms showing below the short sleeves of his gray T-shirt. His ridiculously handsome jaw was blurred by unshaved whiskers, and his dark eyes—visible in the few minutes when he pulled off his sunglasses—were clearly bloodshot.

He looked like he belonged on the beach sleeping off a bender. And he was still so mouthwateringly handsome that she couldn't keep herself from blathering on about every detail of the properties she was showing him, as if he couldn't see for himself the very things she was pointing out.

It was embarrassing. She was supposed to know the value of keeping quiet when she needed to.

They drove to property number three, only a few minutes later than the time she'd arranged with the owners the day before.

She expected them to be gone from the house by the time they got there, but the sight of the van still sitting in front warned her otherwise.

She hated showing properties when the current occupants were present. It never boded well. Nobody relaxed enough to properly give the house fair consideration. And she had high hopes for this particular listing.

She parked behind the van and looked at Grayson.

He was slouched in the passenger seat, cradling the coffee cup that she suspected was empty, the bill of his cap pulled low over his forehead.

"Why don't I check inside first? I think the owners are still here, and it's probably better if they don't realize *who* is looking at their house. More than once, I've had an owner try to drive up the price just because they think they've got a big fish on the hook."

He sent her a faint smile. "You're the expert."

That's what her business cards implied. But driving around "The Grayson" all morning—particularly after his name had been bandied about every fifteen minutes on the local morning news—was leaving her feeling more shaky than confident.

She grabbed her business cards and darted up the front steps to ring the doorbell.

The door opened so immediately, she suspected the owner had been waiting right behind it. "Good morning, Mr. Orchess." She stuck out her business card. "I'm Billie Pemberton with Austin Elite Real Estate. We spoke on the phone yesterday?"

The gray-haired owner smiled. "Come on in, little lady. Can't wait to show off my place here to you and your client." He made no secret that he was trying to see who was in her car parked behind the van, and she was glad for the tinted windows that gave no hint whether anyone was inside the vehicle or not.

"Actually, Mr. Orchess, my schedule has gotten out of hand this morning." It hadn't, but he didn't need to know that. "Is there another time I can bring my client back to see your lovely home?"

The man wrinkled his nose in thought. "Well, the missus and I have to be outta town for the next week or so, so that's out."

Drat, drat, drat. Mr. Orchess was clearly of the mind that he needed to be present, even though she knew very well he had a listing agent representing his multimillion-dollar property. "I don't mind showing your place to my client in your absence if you don't."

"But if I'm not here, I can't tell you all about the special details I've put in myself."

She nodded. "I understand your concern. What if I went through your home now with you and took careful notes? Then I could bring my client back another time and do my best to share all of the special details."

"I s'pose that'd be okay," he said, after giving it some thought.

It took twenty minutes before Billie was able to gracefully leave Mr. Orchess.

Inside, the house was a masterpiece. It also sat on a beautiful piece of property that she thought would be perfect for Grayson.

When she returned to the car Grayson was slouched in the front seat.

Snoring softly.

She almost wished, then, that she hadn't rushed Mr. Orchess quite so much.

She hovered outside the car for a few minutes, sighing. Grayson wasn't the first client to fall asleep on her. Rhonda Dickinson used to fall asleep regularly.

She sincerely hoped that was the only similarity between her new client and Rhonda.

Billie finally climbed behind the wheel of the car, closed the door softly and backed away from the house. Hopefully, he would awaken on his own before they reached the fourth property.

He did not.

Determination filled her. "You are not going to be another Rhonda," she murmured and opened her door. Then pulled it shut again with a loud slam.

Grayson sat up with a start. "What?"

She looked at him innocently. "Property number four is the smallest house we'll be seeing today, but has the most acreage. What do you think so far?"

He pulled off his sunglasses and blinked blearily at her. "I fell asleep."

"Did you? I hadn't noticed."

"I fell asleep with *you* driving."

She wasn't sure what to make of that, except to know

that it wasn't meant as a compliment. "Actually, you fell asleep while I was taking notes about the previous house."

"Thought you didn't notice."

She gave him a look that was hopefully far more congenial than she actually felt, before opening her car door again. "Nearly seventeen acres," she said, as she climbed out. "According to the map, there's a private lake in the middle of it. Do you like boating?"

"Doesn't everybody?" He grabbed a water bottle and seemed to stumble a little as he got out of the car. He swore softly.

She pretended not to see. "I've never been on a boat, myself." She headed for the front door of the house. She'd been through it once already with another client, so didn't have to hunt for the location of the lockbox.

"You've never been on a boat?"

"Nope." She crouched down and entered her access code. The box popped open and she pulled out the house key. "I don't swim." She straightened and smoothed down her skirt. "It doesn't make me a freak."

"Did I say it did?"

"No, but you'd be one of the few who didn't." Max was always riding her about it. She unlocked the door and led the way inside. "Mind the step down when you come in," she warned.

"I see it." He sounded grouchy.

Maybe because he'd just woken up.

Maybe because he was obviously still hungover.

Considering the high hopes she'd had for the morning, things felt on a downhill slide.

She crossed the scuffed wooden floor and opened the wooden shutters so that more natural light filled the living area. "The house was built in 1910, and has undergone a few renovations since. The kitchen has been modernized and two bedrooms were added on in the 1980s."

His expression was unreadable as he wandered around. But at least he didn't look entirely disinterested, as he had with the last house they'd toured. While he headed down the hall toward the bedrooms, she went to the kitchen to leave her business card on the counter. She gave him some time to explore on his own, then slowly followed.

She found him in the master bedroom.

"This one of the modernizations you mentioned?" He pointed his thumb upward toward the ceiling mirror positioned directly over the enormous bed.

Billie felt her cheeks heat. How she could have forgotten about that detail was beyond her. "Actually, the mirror dates back to the original house."

His lips twitched. "Interesting design choice."

"Better or worse than a purple horse?"

He slid his sunglasses down until his brown eyes met hers. "Now, darlin', do you really want me to answer that?"

She straightened her shoulders and channeled her mom's sternest expression. "Perhaps not."

He laughed softly. Which made mincemeat out of all of her channeling and straightening. Didn't matter in the least that he was a client and completely off-limits. Not to mention completely out of her league. He ruffled her.

She edged her way out of the bedroom. "Would you like to see the outbuildings?"

He seemed to consider it for half a minute. Then nodded slowly. "Yeah. I would."

It was more than she'd expected. And her enthusiasm for the morning came back brighter than ever. "All right, then. If you'd like to follow me…"

"Nothing I'd rather do, darlin'."

Chapter Four

"Come on. You can tell Uncle Grayson."

Billie rolled her eyes. "You're not my uncle."

His smile flashed and warmth filled her.

They'd seen two more houses after the one with the mirrored master bedroom and now they were sitting on the grass in a park not far from where she'd grown up.

All because Grayson had seen the circle of food trucks parked there and had decided he was starving.

Which was why she had her legs tucked to one side of her, with a huge paper napkin draped over her thighs to protect herself from the poutine she was eating. Because, evidently, she didn't know how to say no to him very convincingly.

"Okay, so I'm not your uncle. But you can still tell me."

She sighed around another bite of gravy-covered french fry. "This stuff ought to be illegal," she murmured, licking her finger. More to the point, *Grayson* ought to be illegal. "Why are you even interested?"

He pointed over her shoulder at the school field behind them. "You just told me you went to high school right there. That you ran track on that very field. You got me curious. So why not tell me what kind of student you were?"

"I told you I ran track. That's not enough?"

"I can imagine it, too. All long legs and big eyes and hair flying in the breeze."

She rolled her eyes, determined not to let his flirtatious words get to her. How he'd already gotten her to talk about herself was beyond her.

One minute they'd been discussing the merits of the sixth property they'd visited—namely, the accessibility of the acreage where he'd be keeping his livestock. The next thing she knew, he was buying her poutine—overriding her insistence that she pay for her own lunch—and getting her to talk about what it had been like growing up in Austin.

"I was an average student," she finally said, feeling more than a little exasperated. Mostly at herself. Because whether he was offering ridiculously flirtatious statements or not, the man definitely *got* to her. "Average in every single way."

"I find that hard to believe." He'd polished off his own double serving of poutine—which had come with a heart attack–sized serving of bacon atop the cheese curds and gravy—and was sucking down his chocolate milkshake. "There's nothing average about you. Tell me the real truth."

"That *is* the truth. I graduated smack-dab in the middle of my class from that high school over there."

"Then you ended up with a degree in economics from

Rice and are now working at the most prestigious real estate firm in the city."

She flushed. "How do you know I graduated from Rice?"

He tipped down his sunglasses and his warm brown eyes glided over her face. "I looked at your profile on the company's website."

Of course. Silly of her. She was glad that the newness of her college degree wasn't available online. The truth was, she'd gotten her real estate license well before she'd managed to finish her college degree. Mostly because she'd seen the kind of money to be made when she'd worked as a receptionist at Fortunado Real Estate in Houston, helping to pay her way through school.

"From what I saw on the site, you've got some hefty credentials."

"And I'm still the new kid on the block where my boss at Austin Elite is concerned." Then she wanted to kick herself. What good did it do to tell her *client* that? Why couldn't she tell Grayson about the deals she *had* closed? The kind of deals—Rhonda Dickinson aside— that were the reason DeForest Allen had hired her in the first place. "Speaking of my boss, he's going to ask how today went in terms of finding you the perfect property."

"Your boss with his strict code of ethics. What does that mean, exactly?"

If Grayson were anyone else, she wouldn't have even thought to mention Mr. Allen's rules that first day. But she had, so answering as if it was no big deal was the only course she could think to take.

She shrugged, supremely casual. "He discourages involvements between agents and clients."

Grayson's lips twitched. "What kind of involvements?"

She lifted her chin slightly, determined to keep her

wits about her. "Romantic involvements." She didn't allow a beat before returning to her original point. "So what should I say when he asks what kind of progress we made?"

He still looked amused. "Tell him it's a process."

Which told *her* nothing. Except that Grayson wasn't in love with anything she'd shown him that day. If he were, she had no doubt that he'd have said so.

She shifted restlessly on the grass and stretched her legs out in front of her. She should have taken off her pumps to save the high heels from sinking into the soft ground, but she had been afraid of being too casual.

Chowing down on poutine the way they were was bad enough.

"Break it down for me." He obviously wasn't going to let *his* original matter go, either. "What takes an *average*—" he air-quoted the word "—high school girl from point A to point B? Why real estate?"

She thought about lying, but she'd never been good at it. Which meant now would be a terrible time to start. "Know what it's like being the youngest of five kids?" She didn't wait for an answer. "Let's just say I got tired of hand-me-downs."

"So money drives you."

"That makes me sound very calculating." She nibbled her way through a french fry. "I prefer to think that financial security drives me. I've been fortunate. I worked at a very successful firm in Houston. First as a receptionist. Then as an agent. It helped give me a leg up."

"Not that I'm complaining, but what brought you back to Austin from Houston? Would have thought you'd have more business there with the larger population."

"Financial security is great," she admitted honestly,

"but ultimately, I came home to Austin because it's where my family is."

"Roots turned out to be stronger than you thought?"

She nodded, smiling ruefully. "Both my parents will be retiring soon. They drive me crazy sometimes, but yes. Those roots are strong."

"What do your siblings do? Are you close?"

"Two are schoolteachers like my parents. One is a stay-at-home mom. One is a social worker. That's Maggie. She's the next youngest to me, even though there's nearly ten years between us. My brother Ray is the oldest—he's only four years older than Maggie."

He grinned. "And surprise, along comes Billie?"

"Pretty much." Along came Billie…unplanned and the odd duck out for wanting a career that didn't come wrapped in do-gooder ribbon.

She focused on Grayson. "What were *you* like in high school?"

He grinned. "A hell-raiser. We all were."

"All?"

"Two brothers."

"Older or younger?"

"Same. We're triplets. You going to finish that?"

She realized he was eyeing her poutine. "Ah, no. I'm already stuffed."

He grabbed it and started in on the gravy-covered concoction. If she hadn't already seen how much her cousin Max could eat in one sitting, she might have been shocked by the amount of food that Grayson could put away. When it came to rodeo events, steer wrestling was known as the "big man's sport." And Grayson was big, but there wasn't an inch of spare weight anywhere that she could see.

She realized she was staring at his muscular shoulders

and quickly focused elsewhere. "You're one of triplets? That's not something I hear every day."

"We kept my mother busy, that's for sure."

"What about your dad?"

His expression didn't change, but she still sensed that she'd stepped into a conversational pile of doggy doo. "Never knew him. Left my mom high and dry before we were born."

Billie chewed the inside of her cheek. "I'm sorry. I should know better than to make assumptions."

"No reason to be sorry." He looked beyond her again. Along with the food he was voraciously consuming, his bloodshot eyes had cleared. "We had the only parent around who mattered."

It felt like a very good time to change the subject. "Did your brothers get into rodeo, as well?"

His smile returned immediately. "Hell no." His gaze roved over her face as he licked his thumb.

She suddenly felt as gooey inside as the poutine.

"Jayden was interested in getting out of Paseo, but not for every other weekend when there was a rodeo somewhere. He wanted long-term distance."

She frowned at the name of the tiny town. As an agent, she took personal pride in knowing the names of most every town, nook and cranny in the state. Which, considering the size of Texas, was no small feat. And Paseo truly was a tiny map-dot of a town. "You lived in Paseo?" She'd been certain she'd read somewhere that he was from Dallas. Of course, she'd also read somewhere that his name was Grayson Smith.

"Born and raised. Ever been?"

She shook her head.

"Most people haven't. Anyway, after a couple years of college to satisfy our mother, Jayden enlisted in the army. Got out a few years ago. Nathan took a similar path. Navy. He's out now, too. Do-gooders, both of them. Though they'll deny it still to this day."

She couldn't help smiling. "And you?"

He grinned and she felt the impact of it straight down to her core. "I didn't worry about doing good, darlin'. I was just good at...*doing*."

She kept her composure, though it was darned hard. The man was too sexy by far, and he knew it. "And so, *so* modest about it, too."

His smile widened. "You blush very easily."

A comment that made her cheeks turn hotter.

"And you clearly excel at teasing," she said tartly. "Did you start right out with bulldogging?"

"Either you've done your research or you know more about rodeo than I thought. Not everyone knows that's what we call steer wrestling."

She also knew steer wrestling was considered the fastest of the rodeo events, and that Grayson had set records—only to turn around and break those, too. She knew that he'd once competed in other events as well, namely saddle bronc riding and tie-down roping. That he'd been All-Around World Champion more than once, until he'd settled into just steer wrestling several years ago, after suffering some injuries during the Nationals in Las Vegas.

But to admit she knew all that?

She managed a casual shrug. "I told you that my family's big into lots of sports. Not a weekend goes by at my folks' place when there's not someone glued to the TV they set up in the backyard. But as it happens, when I was a student at that school—" she jerked her head toward the field behind her "—I did my share of volunteering at Rodeo Austin." Right alongside Max. "I picked up a few things."

"No kidding." He looked intrigued. "Volunteered doing what?"

"Shoveling a lot of horse pucky," she said wryly. "I tried my hand at barrel racing for a time but it never really stuck. Don't think it would have even if we could have afforded a horse of my own. I, uh, I think I saw you compete once, even." *Think?* If Billie wasn't careful, she'd be telling him about the calendar that he'd once autographed for her. The calendar that she still had.

And because she was afraid of that very thing, she made a point of looking at her watch. But what she saw genuinely surprised her. "I had no idea it was so late." When she'd made the appointment with Grayson the day before, they'd allotted only the morning hours. And it was well into the afternoon. "I'm afraid I've been greedy with your time."

"Pretty sure I'm the greedy one, darlin'." But he reached over and wrapped his long, sinewy fingers around her wrist and looked at her watch himself.

She tucked her tongue between her teeth and tried not to quiver.

"Damn." He sat up straighter. "It is late." He resettled his ball cap before gathering up their trash. "Can I borrow your cell phone? I need to make a call."

"Of course." She was surprised he didn't have one of his own. "It's still in my car. I'll get it."

"Thanks." He took her hand and pulled her so easily to her feet that her nose nearly grazed his chest.

She quickly crossed the grass, feeling her heels sink into the moist dirt with every step.

They were red suede. Not even real suede, and they'd never recover. But if she could get Grayson to close the deal on a property—any property—she'd consider the loss of the shoes well worth it. She reached the car and retrieved her cell phone, only to realize that Grayson had followed her to the car. He took the phone and quickly dialed.

"It's me," he said a moment later. "I'm running late, but you'll have to wait with the I-told-you-sos. We'll have to meet at the library. What's the address?" He'd paced away a few feet from Billie, but he suddenly looked her way. "Got a pen?"

She ducked into the car and retrieved a pen and paper.

He set the latter on the roof of the car. "Okay, repeat that." He scrawled the information on the sheet. "Yeah, I need clothes. My hat and my electric razor. Yep. Yep. I *know.* I'll be in a dark gray gunboat of a car. License plate B-P-REAL." He clicked off the phone and handed it back to Billie. "I'm not going to live this down anytime soon, I'm afraid."

She decided she was more curious than offended at his description of her car. "Live what down?"

"Being late." He held up the paper. His handwriting was bold and slanted, but clear. "Is that far?"

She thought for a moment. "That's the new library complex across town. Going to take at least twenty minutes if there's no traffic." Considering his grimace, she decided not to point out that there was *always* traffic.

"Can I bribe you into driving me there? Or is that going to land you in *involvement* territory?"

"Mr. Allen's not against us being accommodating."

"S'long as there's no kissing."

He was teasing her and she was *not* going to flush. "There's no bribe needed." She reached to take the paper from him, and their fingers brushed when he didn't immediately release it.

"Seriously, I'll owe you one."

She felt all sorts of warm inside again. She tugged a little harder on the paper and he finally let go of it. "I'll collect when you sign a purchase contract." That would make her boss happiest of all.

"Deal." He opened the passenger door and got inside the car. "At least your lead foot will come in handy getting across town," he said when she had gotten in, too, and fastened her seat belt.

"I do not have a lead foot."

"Pretty as it is, it *is* lead," he said dryly. He pulled his cap farther down his forehead again and made a point of tightening his own seat belt. "Okay, Johnny Racer, let 'er rip."

"There's nothing wrong with my driving," she muttered under her breath as she drove out of the park. Just because she'd gotten a couple speeding tickets over the last few years…

Not that he could possibly know about *them*.

But the damage was done, and she couldn't help but feel self-conscious driving across town to the address he'd written down.

Even though she'd expected bad traffic, by the time they were within a few miles of the library, the streets were entirely congested. "I've never seen it this bad," she murmured, as she switched lanes yet again, trying to inch forward. "Whatever your meeting is, I doubt you'll be the only one who's late."

"It's not a meeting. It's a personal appearance." He was obviously paying close attention to their progress. He pointed toward a multistoried building about a mile away. "Is that the library?"

"Yes."

"Keep watch for a black pickup. She ought to be around here somewhere."

Billie started to smile, thinking he was joking.

This *was* Texas, after all. Pickup trucks were a dime a dozen.

But then he pointed again, this time at an enormous black dually parked on the side of the road. "There she is. Pull over."

There were cars on either side of them, so it took a little doing. By the time Billie drew next to the curb, though, the pickup's driver—a slender, brown-haired woman— had gotten out and was jogging toward them.

Grayson lowered his window and took the bulky bag of stuff the woman shoved in for him. Only then did Billie realize the woman was older than she'd initially appeared.

"Cutting it mighty close, son," she said before sticking her arm through the window and right across his nose. "Appreciate you playing chauffeur for Grayson. Would be pretty embarrassing for us if he didn't show up this afternoon."

Grayson had pulled an electric razor out of the bag of stuff. "Billie Pemberton, my mother, Deborah Fortune."

More than a little bemused, Billie shook the hand the woman was offering. "I'm happy to help, Mrs. Fortune."

"Just Deborah." The woman smiled and pulled back from the car. "Entrance is in the back of the library," she told Grayson. "The press is already there. No doubt hoping for something savory after last night's nonsense, so try to behave."

"Yes, ma'am." Grayson was wielding the buzzing razor over his bristled jaw.

Then Deborah was jogging back to her truck.

And it finally dawned on Billie that the increased traffic was because of *him*.

It was all well and good to assure him that he wasn't the first celebrity client she'd ever had.

Except that she'd been lying through her teeth. Oh, she'd had wealthy clients, to be sure. But not ones who literally stopped up traffic.

Still shaving, he tossed his bag into the back seat. Then he pushed open the car door.

For some reason, panic filled her. "Where are you going?"

"Rear seat." As quickly as he said the words, he'd climbed in the back of the car. "Roll up the windows, would you? Probably be a good idea if nobody catches sight of me like this."

Her fingers shook a little as she pressed the electric buttons. In seconds, the interior of the car was once more dimmed by the tinted windows. She looked over her shoulder at him. "Now what?"

He turned off the razor and ran his fingers over his now-smooth jaw. "Now you get me as close to the back entrance of the library as you can." Evidently satisfied with the shaving job, he tossed the razor down and upended the bag's contents and started yanking off his T-shirt.

She blamed her sluggish brain on the poutine.

The contents of the bag were blue jeans. Boots. Trademark black cowboy hat.

He wasn't sitting in the back seat of her gunboat of a vehicle because he wanted to arrive at his appearance "in style," but because he needed the space to change his clothes.

She jerked around until she was facing forward. But it wasn't fast enough to miss the amused look on his face.

Feeling hot, she abruptly decided against maneuvering her car back into the line of vehicles that wasn't moving anywhere, anyway. Instead, she used the empty parking lane to back up until she could turn down a narrow alley.

But not even the sound of gravel beneath her tires was enough to mask the rustle of clothing from the rear. "Suppose you have to, uh, do this a lot," she said a little too loudly.

"You do, huh?"

She heard the distinctive sound of a zipper and would have closed her eyes if not for the fact that she was driving like a madwoman down a narrow alley.

"At least there's more room back here than the last time I was pulling on my jeans in the back seat of a car."

Despite herself, her gaze flew to the rearview mirror.

The laughter in his eyes captured hers.

You'd think she was still a virgin the way her cheeks felt perpetually heated around him.

She'd reached the end of the alley and quickly shot across the cross street, turning up yet another alley.

"You *do* know where you're going, I hope," he commented calmly. "Seeing as how we seem to be traveling away from the library."

"Short cut." Not by distance, but she was banking on the traffic sticking to actual streets, versus the back alleyways. As long as she didn't encounter a delivery truck or a garbage truck blocking her way, she knew she could make good progress. "In high school, my cousin Max and I delivered pizza around here. We had the best delivery times out of everyone." She cringed, realizing she'd mentioned Max's name.

But common sense reminded her that Grayson had no reason to connect Billie Pemberton's cousin Max with his rodeo competitor Max Vargas.

And Grayson was chuckling, anyway. "Pizza, huh?"

Despite her intentions, her eyes strayed to the rear-view mirror again.

She got an eyeful of bare, tanned chest before he started buttoning up his long-sleeved white shirt. And a moment later, just as she turned up yet another alley, he disappeared from view and suddenly a stocking-clad foot was hanging over the back of her seat while he tried to work on a gleaming cowboy boot.

It was accompanied by a lot of swearing that, surprisingly, had her relaxing a little.

She turned down the last alleyway, having bypassed all the traffic, and was now coming at the library from the opposite direction. She sailed past two television trucks and three police vehicles, nipped through the library's delivery entrance and finally came to a stop near the back door. She'd delivered her client safely to the drop-off point. But there was no sign of the black truck his mother had been driving.

When the car engine died, Grayson grabbed his cowboy hat and raked his fingers through his hair. It was starting to curl up at the ends, which meant it was past time to get it cut, though he wasn't sure when he'd find the time to fit it in.

Then he looked out the windows of Billie's car and was more than a little impressed. "We beat my mother here."

"Unless she parked elsewhere, it would seem so." Billie gave him a quick glance over her shoulder. "Do you, um, need anything else?"

"Jeans are zipped and shirt buttons don't seem to be mismatched, so I guess not." He said it for the pure pleasure of watching her cheeks turn pink. "I really do owe you one." He pushed open the back door of the car. "You want to come inside?"

She hesitated. "Are you sure it would be okay?"

He laughed at that. "Pretty sure." He climbed out and planted his hat on his head, then opened her door for her and held out his hand.

She stared at it. "Maybe I should just go."

"Oh, for God's sake." He reached in and took the keys out of her ignition, then closed his hand around hers. "Come on."

She had to scramble to keep up with him. Which was what he'd intended. He pressed the fob on the keys, locking her vehicle as he crossed to the back entrance of the library.

Deborah pulled up in the truck then, looking more frazzled. "This traffic is nuts," she said, as she joined them. She was carrying a box of the signed head shots. "Guess that's what happens when Grayson and the governor of the great state of Texas decide to show up together for the same event."

Grayson felt Billie's hand suddenly drag against his.

"Governor?" She looked stunned. *"What* is going on here?"

"Nothing," he assured her. But he could see Claudia Decker ahead of them, and knew whatever control he'd had that day was soon to be dust in the wind. She was the governor's sister and was positively gleeful over managing to get the two of them there for the opening of her latest literacy project.

He squeezed Billie's hand before letting go. "Stay with my mother. She'll protect you. And the two of you can figure out when I'm free to meet with you again. Got a rodeo in Coleman this weekend, then a quick trip to Montana for a couple days."

"But—"

"Grayson!" Claudia had reached him and presented

her expensively youthful cheek for his kiss. "I can't thank you enough for doing this for me. We're all set up in the new wing."

He dutifully kissed her cheek and let her lead him away.

But he couldn't keep from looking back toward Billie.

She was standing next to his mother, and for a moment, something strange inside his chest tightened.

Then the governor and his security contingent arrived, and he lost sight of them both.

But it was a long time before that strange feeling faded.

Chapter Five

Max took one of the few remaining cupcakes that Billie had set out on a platter in the middle of the birthday feast. "Your cake-decorating skills are improving."

Trust Max to notice. "I didn't have time to bake them," she admitted. Instead of taking a few hours that afternoon to shop, bake and frost the cupcakes she'd promised to bring, she'd hovered in the wings with Grayson's mom at the library dedication. By the time she'd been able to tear herself away from the fascinating spectacle, she'd gotten caught in rush hour traffic going back across town again. So instead of baking, she'd gotten store-bought.

Billie's mother, Peggy, had already given the cupcakes a disapproving look, but Billie knew that Selena hadn't cared. She was just thirteen. Her parents were perpetually broke which was why Peggy had insisted on hosting the party, and Selena loved everything pink and purple and glittering. And the cupcakes fit the bill perfectly.

Max didn't seem to care now, either. He peeled off the paper lining and swallowed an entire half in one bite. "Must be keeping you busy at your new agency," he said around his mouthful. "That's a good thing."

"I work on commission. It's only good if I close the deals," she said dryly.

Billie's mom brushed by her and began removing empty serving trays from the dining room table. "If you were teaching economics like your father and I planned, you wouldn't have to worry about working on a commission."

Long used to Peggy Pemberton's feelings on the subject, Billie just pinned on a smile and lifted one of the heavy trays out of her mom's hands. "Let me help."

Peggy blew a wisp of gray hair away from her forehead. "It's just so darned hot. We had the air-conditioning guy out last week and he tweaked things a bit, but obviously not enough."

"You need a new unit," Billie said. No amount of tweaking was going to keep the ancient thing alive forever. Fortunately, the birthday party had already spilled out onto the back lawn, because the small house wasn't really designed to accommodate the thirty or so family members who'd been crammed inside it for dinner.

"Yes, well, when it dies completely, we'll get one," Peggy said tartly.

Billie wished she'd held her tongue. The last thing she wanted to get into was another argument with her mother about money. Since she'd started earning real commissions, she'd tried more than once to help her parents with some of their unexpected expenses. And every time, she'd earned her mother's wrath. Peggy just wouldn't believe that Billie's real estate career would stay profitable.

Possibly because it was one of the careers that Selena's folks had both failed at.

She picked up another empty platter and followed her into the small kitchen. "I can wash all of this up. Go on outside with everyone else, Mom. It's cooler."

"There's too much here for one person," Peggy protested.

"Then I'll draft Max into helping."

Her mother's eyebrows shot up. "Oh, sure," she said with a dry laugh. But at least it was a laugh, even though she immediately wrapped an apron around her waist and started rinsing dishes at the sink.

Billie went to the doorway in time to see her cousin shoving another cupcake into his mouth. "Come and help me clean up so Mom can go outside with the others where it's cooler."

He looked at her as if she'd grown a second head.

Behind her, she heard her mother laugh again.

Billie gave up. When it came to her family, some things would never change. She moved her mother away from the sink and squirted liquid soap under the hot running water. To accompany the aging air-conditioning system—or rather to *not* accompany it—was the lack of a dishwasher. Not that there would have been any place to put one in the minuscule kitchen. And as the last remaining kid living at home, Billie had grown up with dishwashing duties.

The first apartment she'd gotten on her own hadn't had a separate bedroom, but she'd made darn sure it had a dishwasher.

"You ever think about living anywhere else, Mom?"

Peggy looked surprised. "You mean, like move back home to Horseback Hollow?"

The fact that—after more than forty years—her

mother still considered Horseback Hollow "home" probably had Billie looking just as surprised as Peggy.

"Your father would never leave this house," she said, before Billie could clarify. "And it's paid for." She narrowed her eyes, looking suspicious. "Are you that desperate for real estate clients that you'd expect us to sell your childhood home and buy something we can't afford just as we're about ready to retire?"

Billie winced. She wasn't sure what was more offensive—her mother thinking she needed to drum up business, or that she would look to her own parents to do so. "I'm not desperate for clients, Mom. In fact, I have a new—" She broke off. On those rare occasions that she spoke about clients with her family, it was only in the general sense. And there was nothing "general" when it came to Grayson Fortune.

"A new what?" Max had entered the kitchen.

Ordinarily, that would be a miracle.

"Client, I assume," Peggy answered. She plunked a stack of plates in the sink in front of Billie and tsked a little, adjusting the water temperature. "It doesn't do any good to wash dishes in cold water."

Long practiced, Billie bit her tongue as the hot water turned nearly scalding. Max, however, caught her gaze and grinned knowingly.

"I still don't know where you inherited this interest in real estate," Peggy said as she headed out of the kitchen, "when you could easily teach economics."

Billie quickly adjusted the water temperature again, flooding the sink with enough cold water that she could stand to put her hands in it. By the time her mom returned with another load of dishes, the sink was full and the water off.

"If I hadn't spent more than twelve hours delivering

you from my very own body, I'd think you were left on the doorstep by strangers." Peggy set the stack next to Billie.

It was definitely time to change the subject. "Max, what did you end up bringing Selena for her birthday?"

He made a face. "Only thing she begged me for was an autographed photograph from *The* Grayson."

The plate in Billie's hand slid out of her fingers back into the water, sending soapsuds cascading over the front of her.

"For goodness sake, Billie. Be a little careful! That's my grandmother's china."

Billie lifted the unharmed plate to show her mother, though she was focused on her cousin. "*You* got an autographed photograph from Grayson For—" She bit off the rest of his name, scrambling a little. "For Selena? I thought you hated the guy."

"Well, I damn sure didn't *pay* him for the thing. Guy's not getting any of my hard-earned money."

Peggy looked appalled. "Max, tell me that you didn't forge his autograph!"

"Didn't need to, Aunt Peg. Guy's got stacks of signed pics just lying around if you know where to look."

Photographs like the ones that had been available that afternoon at the library event?

Peggy was giving Max the same look that she'd been giving her seventh-grade math students for as long as Billie could remember. "Tell me exactly where you got Selena's gift."

Max sent Billie a "help me" look, but she was too curious to be of assistance.

He appeared increasingly harried. "It was Bethany's, all right? She left it behind when she dumped me for that cocky old bastard. She obviously doesn't need the picture now that she's got the real thing."

Billie refocused on scrubbing plates. She was increasingly doubtful that Max's feckless barrel racer "had" Grayson at all. Admittedly, she'd spent just one day with him, but the only woman he'd spoken of had been his mother. "I don't think Grayson is old." Or cocky.

"Don't tell me you're still crushin' on him? You made me wait in line with you for two hours back in the day for that dang calendar he signed. You know he still prints 'em?" Max made a face. "Greedy son of a gun, if you ask me. All he's about is making money and collecting other people's girls."

"I'm not crushin' on anyone." And she knew for a fact that Grayson donated all the money he earned from those calendars because the governor had talked about it that very afternoon.

None of which she could tell Max without him flying off the handle.

"You need to forget that Bethany," Peggy said tartly. "She was too old for you, anyway. Focus on meeting a nice girl to marry. Someone who'll give you lots of babies."

"Aunt Peg!" Max's horror was comical. "I don't have t'worry about all that for years yet."

"By the time Hal and I were your age, we already had two children." Peggy pointed her finger in Max's face. "And your mama had one on the way when *she* was twenty-four." Her pointing finger took aim at Billie. "I don't know why the two of you are so resistant to settling down."

"And I don't know why you and my ma are so insistent that we do." Max grinned and slid his arm around Peggy's slender waist. "Don't you have too many grandchildren already?"

Peggy's expression softened slightly. She'd always had more of a tender spot for her sister's youngest than she'd had for her own. "You obviously don't know that there can never be too many grandchildren."

Billie turned on the water to rinse the plates. "As long as you don't expect them anytime soon from me," she muttered under the sound of the water.

"I heard that, Belinda Marie. One of these days you'll fall in love, and you're going to eat those words. I know all about this life plan you think you have laid out for yourself, and I'm here to tell you that it doesn't work that way." Peggy pulled off her apron and tossed it on the cluttered kitchen counter. "Right now, you can just think about that while you take care of all this mess on your own, after all."

Max started to follow Peggy out of the kitchen.

Billie threw the wet dishcloth at her cousin's back. "Hey! Where are you going?"

He grinned, not slowing a bit. "You heard your mama. You can just think about that, Belinda Marie."

She looked back at the dozens of dishes yet to be washed and huffed out a sigh. "Only thing I'm going to think about is my very nice dishwasher at home," she muttered.

Her dishwasher.

And Grayson Fortune.

Two weeks later, Billie stood next to Grayson, looking at an enormous barn. "So, what do you think?"

It was the third time now that they'd been out to view properties, and after failing to catch his interest the last time, when they'd met to go back to the Orchess listing plus three others, she'd decided it was time to take a different tack.

Namely, *not* showing him the actual house until after he'd seen everything else the listing had to offer.

Despite his intention to purchase a new home, she could tell he wasn't quite ready to see himself living in any of them. But when it came to barns and good grazing land and accessibility and water? Those things he did care about.

She'd also realized that he didn't give two figs about her carefully prepared folios, which were generally so important to her other clients. She wasn't used to it, but it did save her a fair amount of preparation time. Which was a good thing, given his unpredictable schedule.

"When was the barn built?"

She scanned the information sheet she had printed out for herself. She didn't have a lot of confidence that he'd like the Harmon ranch, because it was so much more expensive than anything he'd expressed an interest in seeing before. It was also considerably farther away from the city and came with nearly a hundred acres. Yes, he'd said he wanted acreage, but this was on another scale entirely. But DeForest Allen had brought the new listing to her attention after the status meeting that morning. And so here they were. "The barn was built three years ago."

"It's not bad." He tucked his sunglasses in the collar of his navy blue T-shirt and thumbed back his black cowboy hat as he surveyed the acreage all around them. "It's on well water, you said?"

"Yes." Fortunately, she'd also gotten over the worst of her tendency to chatter nervously when she was around him, and she was able to leave it at that. She'd realized that when Grayson had questions, he asked them. And now, she was determined to remain quiet, leaving him to make his own observations.

On the *un*fortunate front, she was realizing that left her with plenty of time to just observe *him*.

And the more she observed, the more disturbed she felt. Because she genuinely liked him.

Liked him in a way that set all her nerves on edge.

Frankly, she blamed her mother.

Ever since Selena's party, when Peggy had harped on falling in love, Billie hadn't been able to get Grayson out of her head. Which would have been fine if all she'd been thinking about was finding him a property that he couldn't resist.

"Billie?"

She realized she'd completely missed whatever it was he'd said. She rustled the papers she was holding as if to blame her inattention on them. "Sorry?"

"The land does come *with* the house, doesn't it?" He'd taken off his cowboy hat and used it to gesture at the multiwinged stone structure.

She pretended her cheeks weren't hot. "Of course. The, uh, the house was built twenty years ago, but it was evidently renovated about the same time they built the barn." She quickly started toward the dwelling and eventually he fell in step with her. In the silence of the afternoon, their footsteps seemed loud as they crossed the brick-paved courtyard between the oversize barn and the mansion-sized house.

He resettled his hat on his head. "You seem distracted today."

"Do I?" She opened the lockbox. But the house key that was supposed to be inside wasn't there.

She frowned and pulled off her sunglasses, glancing around her. She wasn't so distracted that she would have accidentally tipped out the key without noticing, was she?

Grayson stopped next to her and his arm lightly grazed hers. "Something wrong?"

"Key's missing." She was already pulling out her cell phone. "I need to report it." Each time agents entered their unique code on the digital lockbox, the information was recorded. So it would be easy enough to determine who'd been there last. Plus, Billie wanted to make sure *she* wasn't blamed for the lapse.

Grayson didn't look particularly perturbed. "While you do that, I'm going to walk around and look in the windows."

It was apparent that they weren't going to be able to get inside anytime soon, so if he didn't like what he saw through the windows, they wouldn't need to waste time trying to come back.

She left a message with the listing agent about the key situation, closed up the lockbox again and went to find Grayson.

He was sitting on the built-up stone side of the glittering blue pool located at the rear of the house. His long legs were extended, boots crossed at the ankles.

"I left a message about the key." She slid her sunglasses back on. "We might as well head on to the next listing."

He patted the wide ledge beside him. "Sit."

She hesitated for half a second before complying. The stone was hot through the fabric of her skirt. But no hotter than the feel of him, even though she'd left a healthy space between them.

She shuffled her papers on her lap. "It's going to take us at least an hour to drive to the next listing. The asking price is definitely too high, but I've heard the owner is getting anxious, so I believe there will be some real negotiating room if it turns out to be the right property for you."

"What's wrong?"

Her shoulders felt stiff. "Nothing's wrong. Except for a missing key throwing a crimp in my plans."

He uncrossed his ankles and cupped his hand around the edge of the stone tile separating them. "Look, I know I'm not the easiest of clients."

She pushed to her feet, smoothing down her skirt self-consciously. "Don't say that. You've been an ideal client." Aside from the first day when he'd been hungover, his limited availability and his propensity to turn up his handsome nose at every sales listing she suggested, he was actually one of the easier clients she'd had. It wasn't his fault that she'd been having dreams about him. Day-dreams. Night dreams. Evidently, her overactive imagination didn't discriminate when it came to hours of the day.

"Even though I haven't found anything that says *home* the second we walk through the door?"

She squelched a sigh. "Some would say that's my failure, not yours." Some *had* said it. Namely, her boss at the meeting that morning. Fortunately, DeForest Allen wasn't a mind reader or he'd have also delivered a lecture on the importance of recognizing the fine line between making accommodations for an important client and being *too* accommodating.

"Grayson, we'll find the right fit for you. It's not as though you're looking to purchase a three-bedroom tract home. It just takes time."

"Time that I haven't given you much of. At least not since our first date."

There was no point in shivering over the word, when she knew good and well that he didn't mean "date" date. He just meant their first day of home touring. "I knew from the beginning that you have a tight schedule. Frankly, I was surprised you were even available today."

"Why's that?"

She spread her hands and the papers clutched in her right hand fluttered in the faint breeze. "Reno starts tomorrow. I know you're competing."

He lifted an eyebrow.

"Your mother told me," she added, lest he speculate that she'd been following his schedule out of more personal interest. All right. So she *had* been. But just because she knew he'd won at the Coleman rodeo—much to Max's consternation—then placed in Montana last weekend, and she'd seen his name on the roster for Reno, didn't mean that she needed to divulge the truth. "It's a couple days drive from here." Long days. Last time she'd talked to Max, he'd been on the road midway there. "I guess you must be flying."

"My mother wanted a quick visit home to Paseo before Reno, so my hazer, Lou, and another friend are driving everything out to Nevada for us. Her flight to Reno was this morning. Mine is tonight."

Considering his expression, he didn't look too happy about it. "Didn't you want to go to Paseo, too?"

"I had business to take care of here."

"Grayson Gear business?"

"Billie Pemberton business."

Her mouth went more than a little dry. She reminded herself that what he really meant was real estate business. Which, if he'd rather have been visiting home, might explain his discontented expression. She nudged up her sunglasses again. "Well, while I do have you, we should probably make our way to the next place instead of wasting time sitting here in the hot sun."

"It is hot. And humid." He looked over his shoulder at the glittering swimming pool. "Too bad you don't swim.

We could sneak in a dip." He gave her a quick look. "I could teach you how to swim."

He could teach you lots of things.

She kicked the sneaky voice inside her head right to the curb. "In someone else's pool?"

"Without their knowledge even." His expression had lightened and his lips twitched. "Lends a certain air of excitement, don't you think?"

"Lends a certain air of getting my rear end fired," she corrected. Getting just that right amount of dryness in her voice should have earned her an acting award.

"Only if your uptight boss found out."

"I should never have told you about that."

"Why?"

"Because it's not relevant."

Even with her sunglasses, his gaze trapped hers. "It's not?"

She felt a bead of perspiration slide down her spine. She swallowed and moistened her lips. "In any case, he's not going to find out for the simple reason that we're not getting in that pool. We don't even have swimming suits." She regretted the words as soon as she said them.

Because, naturally, Grayson's perfectly shaped lips spread slowly into a sexy-as-hell grin. "Well, hell, darlin', as far as I'm concerned, that ain't really a problem."

At this rate, she wasn't getting any closer to him signing a purchase contract. Instead, she was getting a whole lot closer to losing her willpower where he was concerned. Which was the height of stupidity. He flirted because it was his nature to flirt with *any* female.

She shook her papers at him. "We have places to go, Grayson."

"Fine." But he cupped his fingers in the pool and flipped water toward her.

She jumped back, but not quickly enough to evade the splash. She stared down at her thin silk blouse, which had started the day as a pristine white, but was now clinging almost transparently to her lace bra. She plucked the wet fabric away from her chest. "I can't believe you did that!"

He laughed. "Considering the way you drive, I can't believe you moved so slowly."

She was torn between embarrassment and the desire to laugh, herself. Even if the pool water ruined her blouse, the water did feel refreshing. And Grayson's laugh was low and sexy as all get-out. The sound of it made every nerve inside her tingle.

She crossed her arms and channeled her mother's best humorless glare, though it was difficult. "It's time to go, Grayson."

He made a face, but finally pushed off the ledge. "Did I tell you that the first crush I ever had on a woman was my third grade teacher, Miss Frost? She always used to cross her arms and give me that sort of look, too."

"If you're saying that to unnerve me, it won't work." Liar, liar, pants on fire.

"Just having a conversation, darlin'." He passed by her. "Your papers are wet, by the way."

"Gee. I wonder why." She waited until his back was turned, then dropped the wet pages and scooped both her hands into the pool water and flung it at him.

She was nowhere near as effective at it as he had been, but she did manage to douse the back of his shirt pretty well.

Enough for him to turn on a dime, giving her a surprised look.

She laughed.

He took a step toward the pool's edge. "Now you've done it."

She had the sense to be a bit alarmed and started to step away.

He dunked his arm in the pool and sloshed a wave of water toward her. It sluiced over the wide rock ledge, splashing her in the face and flooding over the toes of her shoes.

"That's three pairs of suede shoes I've ruined now because of you," she said, blinking against the water droplets. The second pair had fallen victim to the cow pie she'd accidentally stepped into while Grayson decided the Orchess land wasn't right for him, either.

"You don't swim," he reminded her as she leaned over the pool ledge.

"Doesn't mean I'm afraid of water." She sliced her arm across the surface, sending a jet of spray his way.

He took the water full frontal. He slowly pulled off his hat, and his smile flashed almost as bright as the beating sun. "Oh now, darlin', all bets are off."

She braced herself as he dipped his hat toward the pool. "Grayson..."

And then his hat filled with water and all bets were off, indeed.

Chapter Six

"Here." Billie handed Grayson a bath towel. "You're still dripping."

It was an exaggeration, but Grayson let it pass because he was preoccupied looking around Billie's starkly furnished apartment. She'd suggested dropping him off at his hotel, until he'd told her he'd already checked out that morning.

She hadn't been quite able to hide her consternation, then, as she'd brought him back to her place.

Far as he was concerned, they might as well have taken an illicit dip in that swimming pool. They'd ended up as wet as if they'd jumped in fully clothed. But they'd left a good portion of that moisture behind on Billie's car seats during the long drive back to Austin.

He flipped the towel around his neck and absently unbuttoned his clinging shirt as he approached the oversize windows that afforded Billie a decent view of the river.

Considering the location of the apartment building, it didn't take a genius to guess she was paying a hefty price tag for that particular view. It was almost as good as the view from his usual penthouse hotel suite. She even had a balcony furnished with a small, cushioned couch, a chair and a low, tiled table. Sitting on the table was a shallow wicker basket holding a couple glossy magazines.

The inside of the apartment wasn't quite so well equipped. Not unless she had a couch hiding in the brown cardboard packing boxes that were stacked against one wall. Aside from them, she had a dining room table with four chairs, a television that was sitting on the floor, and one leather chair.

He glanced at her. She was standing in the kitchen, but had kicked off her shoes in the tiled foyer.

It dawned on him then that he hadn't seen her without shoes until now. "You're short."

She paused in the act of twisting her wet hair up in a white towel, turban-like. "You're so good for my ego," she muttered and then straightened.

He wondered what her ego would feel like if he admitted that every time he looked at her, he wanted her. Too young for him or not, he wanted her. And it was a problem that kept getting worse. His stunt with the pool definitely wasn't helping things. "You're always wearing high heels," he said casually.

She returned to the foyer to pick up her discarded shoes. "Considering I seem to ruin a pair every time I take you out for a home tour, I'd do better to switch to rubber muck boots." She pointed the shoes at him. They'd been a brilliant peacock blue until the chlorinated pool water had had its way with them. Now they were splotched blue and white. "I'll be back in a minute."

She set the shoes on the kitchen counter next to his wet

hat before heading across the dark wood floor to disappear behind a door at the end of the short hall.

Where, no doubt, she would change out of her wet clothes.

He looked back at the window and lightly thumped his forehead against the glass. "Dumb move, Gray."

Then he realized the windows were actually sliding doors, and after a second of hunting, he released the lock and slid one of the panels open, then stepped out. The afternoon sun was hotter than ever, but it didn't quite reach all the way across Billie's balcony. He closed the patio door behind him and shrugged out of his shirt and spread it across the back of the side chair. Then he sat on the couch and studied his Castletons. They'd fared better than Billie's shoes, but then they were working boots meant to withstand some punishment.

He still had several hours yet before he had to catch his flight to Reno. His shirt would be dry for sure by then. As for his jeans...

He stretched out his legs across the entire depth of the small balcony. His jeans would have to dry *on* his stupid ass.

He hadn't been sitting there five minutes when he heard the door slide open.

"Here." Billie held out a tall glass. "Don't worry. It's plain old iced tea. No chai. No spice. Nothing but grocery store orange pekoe. No lemon, either, because I'm out."

He'd automatically wrapped his fingers around the glass. But she didn't immediately release it.

"Unless you prefer cucumber-and-basil-infused water." A faint smile played around her lips.

He chuckled. "Not in this lifetime. Tea's fine. Thanks."

She released the glass and after a hesitation that he might have imagined, set aside the magazine basket and moved his shirt from the side chair to spread it out over the low table. "I do have a dryer," she said, sounding unusually diffident. "If you want to, um, dry your clothes in it."

"Sunshine and heat'll do."

She sat down in the chair and sipped her own glass of tea.

She'd changed into a faded blue T-shirt that said Rice across her breasts and a pair of shorts that exposed less leg than her usual short skirts. The towel was gone, and her hair hung in a damp-looking braid over one shoulder.

She looked about thirteen years old.

Except for the curves under Rice, that was.

He looked away, but his gaze landed on the magazines inside her wicker basket. An image of Ben Robinson was on the cover of the top one. Ben *Fortune* Robinson. A *legitimate* heir of Gerald Robinson.

And Grayson's half brother.

He stifled a sigh and focused on the ice cubes bobbing in his tea. "Why economics?"

"Excuse me?"

"Why'd you get a degree in economics?"

"My father teaches economics."

"So, following in his footsteps?"

"That's what my parents planned, anyway. They're not exactly thrilled with my real estate career choice." Her lip twisted as she took a sip of tea.

He gestured, taking in the balcony and view. "If it means you can pay for an address like this, what's the problem?"

"It's not what they had planned for me. You know how parents can be when they make plans for their children."

"Only things my mom keeps making plans for these days are grandchildren."

Billie smiled then. "A common affliction I am very familiar with, actually. My mother already has half a dozen grandchildren, but she thinks I'm disregarding my duties by not increasing their numbers." Seeming to relax, she stretched out her slender legs until she could prop her heels on the corner of the table next to his shirt.

Her toenails were painted in brilliant red. And she had a narrow black ring around her middle toe.

Then he looked closer, not caring that he was pretty much staring. It wasn't a plain black ring. It was a delicate, filigree design. "Is that a tattoo?"

She curled her toes, as if she wanted to hide the evidence. Her brown eyes skated over him, then away. "Yes."

He smiled slightly. "Well, you're just full of surprises, Rice."

Her cheeks were pink.

He supposed it might be because of the heat, but he doubted it.

"I got it when I turned twenty." She wriggled her toes again. "Seems silly now."

"Because…?"

"Tattoo on a toe? Hurt like the dickens." She shrugged. "But I was trying to impress a guy and I was young and stupid. Fortunately, I got over the habit."

He couldn't help chuckling. "Darlin', you may not be stupid but you're *still* young."

"You say that like you're ancient."

"And your point?"

She gave a huffing laugh. "Obviously, you're not."

"I've got thirteen years and a lotta miles on you, darlin'."

She rolled her eyes and sat forward to grab the glossy magazine from the basket. She flipped it open and waved it at him, tapping the photograph of him from the finals of Rodeo Austin. "And that's why *Weird Life Magazine* just named you one of the most eligible bachelors in Texas for the third time running. Because you've got so many miles on you." She closed the magazine and tossed it onto the cushion beside him. "Every time you come to my office, you send half the women there into palpitations."

"Only half?"

She chuckled, shaking her head. "You know good and well what your own appeal is. You don't need me stroking your ego."

"I could think of a few other things." He waited a beat, enjoying the way her cheeks turned red, then fed her own words back to her. "But that's not relevant."

Her eyes flew to his, then skittered away.

He changed tack. "What happened to the guy? The tattoo guy. Was he impressed?"

She spread her hands slightly, seeming to relax a little. "Briefly."

"No tears? No broken heart?"

Her lips curved ruefully as she shook her head. "Neither his nor mine."

"Ever had one?"

Her chin angled. "Have *you*?"

"Hell yeah. Miss Frost ruined me for years."

She laughed. When it faded, she looked reflective as she toyed with her braid. "I don't think I have ever cried over a guy. Much less had a broken heart. Disappointed heart?" She made a face. "That's pretty typical. My friends all think I'm a cynic."

"Are they right?"

Her shoulders shrugged. "Maybe. I don't know. I just know it's easier to focus on my work than my personal life. I like being able to depend on myself. If *I* let me down, it's my own darn problem."

He studied her for a long moment. "I doubt that happens too often."

Her lashes swept down. Her cheeks looked pink again.

He shifted, and the magazine slid off the couch. He picked it up, closed it and tossed it back into the wicker basket.

"I didn't graduate from college," he admitted abruptly, though he wasn't real sure why. Maybe because of that photograph of his übersuccessful half brother on the cover. The half brother he'd so far refused to meet. Even though both Jayden and Nate told him that Ben—as well as all the other Robinson siblings—were decent enough people despite having Gerald as a father. "I took classes now and then, but there was never enough time to do the job right. Which means you, young lady, are way more educated than I am."

"Grayson Gear is turning record profits and I saw you rubbing arms with the governor." Billie's voice turned dry. "The lack of a college degree doesn't seem to have held you back much."

He grunted. Maybe there was some truth in that. To hear Jayden tell it, Gerald's legitimate kids—all eight of 'em—were educated up the wazoo.

He rubbed at a sudden pain between his eyebrows.

"What kind of classes did you take?" she asked him.

He dropped his hand. Billie was looking at him.

"Agriculture. Animal husbandry." He grimaced. "Marketing."

She smiled slightly. "There's nothing wrong with marketing."

"There is when you're pulling a D in it. Believe me, I wasn't breaking any records when it came to my truncated college education." He bent his knees suddenly and sat forward to grab the magazine back out of the wicker basket. "My sister-in-law used to write for *Weird Life*."

"No kidding? Small world. I sold the publisher's son a house in Houston last year. She doesn't write for them anymore?"

He shook his head. When Ariana met Jayden, she'd been writing a series on "Becoming a Fortune" and had been investigating all the deep dark secrets behind Gerald Fortune Robinson's sexual peccadilloes. More specifically, the results of those peccadilloes. She'd given up the series and her job when she'd fallen for Jayden, but that didn't make the things she'd uncovered go away. They were just being publicly dissected by other members of the media now. Scuttlebutt was that even Gerald's father, Julius Fortune, had been incapable of fidelity.

Made a man wonder if there was a faulty gene in the family. And God knew Grayson had never been interested in committing himself to one woman.

"You know who this is?" He tapped the magazine cover.

"The guy who runs Robinson Tech," Billie answered without hesitation. "Can't own a computer these days without knowing that. Not around these parts, anyway." She sipped her tea. "I helped one of his secretaries find a house my first week at Austin Elite. Nice girl. It was her and her husband's first home purchase. We're closing escrow on it soon."

"That guy's my half brother. We have the same father. Only, good old dad decided to marry *Ben's* mama even though he'd already knocked up mine."

Jesus, Joseph and Mary. He couldn't believe the words had come out of his mouth. What was wrong with him?

He tossed the magazine back in the basket and shoved to his feet. "I need to get moving." He grabbed his still-damp shirt.

Her brows pulled together. "I thought your flight wasn't until this evening."

It wasn't. But he was obviously losing his freaking mind. She stood a lot more slowly than he had, looking wary and bewildered as she set aside her glass of tea. "Grayson—"

"I'll talk to you after Reno. I don't know when that'll be, exactly. Events go all week and it depends how my runs go. If I'll be home early—"

"—or staying through the final short round," she finished for him. "I know how it works."

He wished he could say he knew how his brain was working at the moment. "When I do get to town, I want to go back and see that place we were at today. If it's still available." He pulled open the slider and went inside.

She followed him, practically jogging across the wood floor to keep up with him. He grabbed his hat from the kitchen, and when he reached for the front door handle, she covered his hand with his. "Grayson, slow down. Let me get my shoes at least. I'll drive you to the airport."

"Don't worry about it."

She looked ready to argue.

"I'm supposed to meet up before the flight with an old friend." It was a true enough. He'd gotten an unexpected message at the hotel, though he hadn't intended to follow up on it. "I don't know if you follow barrels still, but maybe you've heard of her. She won last year's final in barrel racing. Lives here in Austin. Bethany Belmont."

Billie was silent for half a second before her slender hand moved away. "Never heard of her." She folded her arms across Rice. "I'll contact your mother about when you can fit in viewing the Harmon ranch." She smiled, though there was no humor in it. "If you want your *friend* to see it, feel free to bring her along."

He'd just dumped the truth in her lap about his being related to Austin's own version of royalty and she was going to be pissy about something as inconsequential as Bethany Belmont? "I think she could care less about it, but who knows?" He pulled open the door. "Sorry about your shoes."

"Get a decent draw?"

Grayson glanced at the young man who'd come up beside him on a good-looking sorrel. It was the first time Max Vargas had addressed him directly in months. "Decent enough." Shortly before their event, the draw had been made for the steer each bulldogger would run that morning.

He lowered the stirrup and swung up into the saddle. Vix shifted slightly, but soon settled, just as Grayson had known he would. "See you're on Deca," he said to Max. "He's a good ride. You been on him before?"

Max shook his head. His black hat was pulled low over his eyes, hiding most of his expression.

"He'll do everything right when you let him do it."

Max's mouth was still visible. It curled with obvious annoyance at Grayson's advice. "I know how to handle him."

Good enough. Max's first go would immediately follow Grayson's. Maybe that was the only point of the brief exchange.

Grayson dismissed the cocky young man from his thoughts as he looked toward his hazer. "You feeling good this morning, Lou?"

"Good as ever." Lou Blackhorn was a bulldogger himself, though he'd been sidelined for a few months as he recovered from an injury. But that didn't stop him from hazing. "Don't go breaking the barrier, now."

Grayson grinned. Long as Lou warned him not to

break the barrier—the breakaway rope stretched across the front of Grayson's box that couldn't be crossed before the steer reached its predetermined head start—he hadn't had a single broken barrier penalty. A bulldogger could have a smokin' fast time throwing down a steer, but it got shot to hell if he got hit with that ten-second penalty.

He rode Vix deep into the box and didn't even need to coax him into backing into the far corner, away from the steer's pen. As usual, he had his two best horses with him, but Vix always ran best first thing in the morning. Van, on the other hand, loved the night lights and crowds.

Grayson sat relaxed and easy in the saddle, but inside, he felt the familiar ripple of nerves. He considered those nerves to be a good thing. If he wasn't nervous, it was guaranteed he wouldn't have a good run.

Despite the fact that their first go was during slack, it was still a crowded affair, with the dozen or so officials and livestock handlers also packed into the area. And inside the metal pen between Grayson's box and Lou's, the steer was huffing noisily.

"Sounds like this ol' boy's anxious to be out this morning, too." The gray-haired man manning the chute grinned at Grayson. He'd wait until he got the nod from Grayson before tripping the lever that released the steer.

"That's the way I like them." He held the reins low and easy, catching Lou's eyes for a second. His blood thrummed in his ears and he looked down the arena for a moment, envisioning his ride. "All right, buddy," he murmured. Vix might not have been one of professional rodeo's horses of the year like Deca, but he was one of Grayson's best. "Let's show 'em how it's done." Then he gave the nod.

After that came the always strange fusion of blur and crystal sharp detail.

The steer bolting from the chute. Lou following a moment later. The snapping sound of the barrier releasing. The launch of horseflesh beneath him, going zero to thirty in the span of a second.

The steer was fast.

Vix was faster.

Then Grayson was sliding from horse toward steer, catching one arm around one of the fast-running beast's horns and wrapping his hand around the other horn.

He felt his heels dig good and deep in the dirt and he wrangled the steer around until the animal was on the ground, four hooves pointing the same direction.

It was textbook perfect.

The moment Gray let the steer go, the animal was back on his feet, chasing around in circles, frisky as all get-out. That's the way it usually went.

Grayson didn't even know what his time was, except that it'd felt decent. Mostly, as he rolled to his feet and brushed the dirt off his hands, he was feeling that immediate satisfaction of knowing he'd just thrown a good steer that was twice his weight. His rib wasn't hurting. His thigh wasn't aching.

If he didn't let himself think about the look on Billie's face when he'd left her apartment the day before, it was pretty much a perfect morning.

"And we're off to a fine start, folks," the announcer was saying. "That's the Big G outta Texas with four-point-two-o-o seconds! Grayson's an old-timer out here, showing all them young bucks how it's done."

There was a smattering of laughter and applause, more from the other bulldoggers and hazers waiting on their go-round than from the small crowd of onlookers sitting in the bleachers around the arena.

Grayson waved his hat once as he jogged to the edge of the arena, where Lou was already waiting with Vix.

"Good run, Gray." Lou handed over the reins.

"Only 'cause you kept that son of a gun where I needed him." He swung up into the saddle again, intending to hang around to see how everyone else did. Plus, Lou had already told him he was hazing for a couple other guys.

Including Max Vargas.

It was a common enough occurrence. A good hazer was worth his weight in gold and typically got a nice cut of the bulldogger's payoff when he was in the money. But out of the dozens of entrants, only a handful would end up in the money. Even when Lou did compete himself, he also did a lot of hazing because he had two ex-wives and four kids he was supporting.

"And up next in the box is Max Vargas," the announcer was drawling, "outta the fine capital of Texas. Max is standing at number seventeen in the world right now and he's on last year's horse of the year, so let's see what he and Deca can do-o-o."

Max's nerves as he and Deca settled back into the corner of the box were easily visible to Grayson. He was holding the reins tight and high. Exactly the way Deca didn't like.

"Come on, Max," Grayson murmured. "Loosen up."

There was no possible way the other man could have heard. Too much distance. Too much noise. Too much distraction.

But Max suddenly rolled his head around. He planted his hat down harder on his head. Then he lightened up the reins and with a nudge of his boot had Deca shimmying sideways back into the corner.

Less than half a minute later, it was all over.

"And *that's* Max Vargas with a four-point-three-e-e,

ladies and gentlemen. And we've got ourselves a fine start here this morning in Reno. Folks, let's not let this cowboy outta the arena without a little love."

Aside from noting the time, Grayson paid little attention to the announcer or the applause he was coaxing from the crowd. Instead, he watched Max say something to Lou that had his old friend's expression tightening before Max stomped out of the arena, leaving his hazer to deal with Deca.

Without thinking too much about it, Grayson casually moved to one side, knowing that he'd be blocking Max's exit if the kid ever looked beyond himself.

"Good time," he said, a second before Max would have plowed over him.

Max's head came up. He glared at Grayson. "Would've been better if my hazer woulda done his job right." His voice was tight and low. "As usual, everyone's loyalty is to *you*."

Grayson clamped his arm around the shorter man's shoulders, pulling him close. "Kid, you've got talent, but you've got a helluva lot to learn if you think a pro like Lou doesn't do his best every single ride no matter how much of an ass you are. You've been at this long enough to know there are three things that matter in bulldogging. You. The steer. And your hazer." He ignored Max's effort to shake him off. "You want a better time? Stop blaming someone else and stop straightening your legs so damn much every time you throw the steer. Standing up that much just adds time on the clock."

"If I wanted your advice, I'd ask." Max shoved his way past Grayson.

He took a step after the kid, only to stop short when he spotted his mother sitting in the stands. He hadn't seen her since arriving in Reno.

She gave him a smile and a thumbs-up.

All normal stuff.

What *wasn't* normal was the glimpse Grayson got of a man sitting about a dozen rows from Deborah who'd just risen and was walking away.

The man wore a ball cap on his head, a dark colored T-shirt and jeans. But Grayson could swear the man was Gerald Robinson.

Grayson's hands curled into fists as he squinted, trying to see the man better before he moved out of sight. But Deborah had risen, too, and was heading down the bleachers toward Grayson.

If she knew the man who'd left her pregnant and abandoned was anywhere near, she gave no sign of it.

And when Grayson looked back to where Robinson had been—if it *had* been Robinson—the man was gone.

His mom's smile seemed perfectly normal when she finally reached him. "Good time." She was carrying a printed list that he knew would be his schedule for the coming week. "How's the rib feel?"

"It's fine. How was Paseo?"

At his abrupt tone, her eyes narrowed. "It was fine."

"Was Robinson there?"

She frowned. "What are you talking about?"

He scanned the arena yet again. "Forget it. Nothing." He plucked the list from her hand and studied it. Autographing session at noon. Conference call at three about Grayson Gear's proposed collaboration with Castleton Boots.

His mom snatched the list back, giving him a close look. "Nothing my fanny."

He exhaled. "It's not unheard of. He's shown his miserable face in Paseo before. As Jerome Fortune, the guy faked his death a long damn time ago and recreated himself as Gerald Robinson. Now that he's found you, who knows what else he's capable of."

"I should think you'd know what *I'm* capable of. Just because I wanted to go home and catch up with my other sons, you start thinking the worst?"

"He's a married man with more kids than he can count."

Temper filled her eyes. "That sounds like you're warning me, son."

"I'm not warning. I'm just… I just don't want him hurting you again."

"Oh, for heaven's sake, Grayson. I was in love with Jerome once, but that was a long time ago. It happened too fast, and maybe if I could turn back time, we could have found our way. But I can't turn it back and I'm no home wrecker. If you're intent on worrying about something, worry about yourself."

"What do I have to worry about?"

"Making more out of your life than work! Finding someone who'll keep your bed warm at night. I mean the *same* someone who'll be there night after night after night. Look at your brothers—"

"I'm not my brothers." He cut her off before she could head on down that road again. Since he'd learned about his biological father, his worst fear was that he'd turn out to be more like Jerome/Gerald than like his own brothers. Neither Jayden nor Nathan had ever shared Grayson's proclivity against entanglements. "Only thing *I* need to worry about is showing up on time where I'm supposed to show up." He tried to take the list from her again. "I'm gonna need that, you know."

She tossed the paper at him, obviously still annoyed. "Autographing and press conference today. Grayson Good session with an elementary school tomorrow and a senior center the next day. I'll work out the rest of the week when we know your next go-round." She waited a beat, studying him closely. "You saw Billie yesterday, didn't you?"

He picked up the list from the ground where it had fallen. "I looked at a *house* yesterday with my real estate agent." Spilled half his guts with her, too.

"With Billie."

He folded the sheet and shoved it in his back pocket. "Dammit, Ma. Would you give it a rest?"

Her eyebrows rose. "I'll give it a rest when you tell me what's really got a burr under your saddle."

He pinched the bridge of his nose. There was no way he was going to tell her he thought he'd seen Robinson in the arena. She'd be upset that he was hallucinating, or upset that he wasn't.

But he was even more reluctant to talk about Billie. It was a guarantee that Deborah would make too much of anything he said. And it was hard enough not thinking about Billie, particularly after the way he'd left.

From the corner of his eye, he saw Max Vargas stomping around, still peeved. It was a toss-up who the young man wished six feet under more—Grayson or Lou, as the hazer passed nearby, still leading Deca.

His mother was still giving him the stink eye and Grayson threw out a Hail Mary. "I saw Bethany Belmont last night before my flight. She's pregnant."

His mother's eyes widened with dismay. "With your—"

"Hell no." He'd never slept with Bethany, even back in the early days, though he'd given it his best shot for a time. "She didn't say who the father was."

Deborah looked confused. "Then why'd she tell you?"

He spread his hands. "I guess she needed someone to talk to. She's got no family. Or maybe because we both grew up in Paseo. Take your pick. You were single and pregnant once." He looked over the bleachers again. "What else should I have done? She asked me for a job at Grayson Gear. She's thirty-six years old and pregnant. She can't compete right now. She's behind on her bills."

His mother's lips compressed. Then she sighed. "Even after all these years, I remember what that's like. What did you tell her?"

"To talk to Jessica on Monday." He'd already told his manager at the company to find a spot for Bethany. "Meanwhile, I gave her about five hundred to tide her over."

"She might use it for an abortion."

"I doubt it. She was anxious about finding a job, but still seemed pretty happy about the baby."

"Hey, mister." The greeting was accompanied by a tug on his shirt and Grayson looked down to see a young boy holding an autograph book and wearing a hopeful expression. "Can I get your autograph?"

Glad for the interruption, Grayson crouched down until he was at the boy's level. He had dark brown hair and dark brown eyes and looked about five. "You bet. What's your name, cowboy?"

The boy beamed. "Billy."

"Billy, eh?" Grayson had always suspected the universe had a strange sense of humor. He took the book and opened it to a blank page. "I knew a Billy a long time ago." That was true enough. "Billy Wood was a great bronc rider. Taught me a lot back in the day. How old are you?"

"Six." The boy preened. "I'm gonna be a mutton buster!"

Grayson smiled as he scrawled his autograph across the page.

"You know, that's how Grayson started," Deborah told the boy. "Mutton busting."

Billy looked at Grayson, awed. "Really?"

"Sure did. But you know, every mutton buster needs a good hat on his head."

The boy rubbed the toe of his scuffed boots in the dirt and looked toward a dark-haired woman standing protectively nearby. "My mama said I could get boots or a hat but not both."

"My mama used to tell me the same thing." Grayson smiled at Billy's mom as he returned the autograph book. Then he took his hat and plunked it on the boy's head. "Hold on to that, cowboy. One day it'll fit you just fine."

Billy's eyes widened like saucers. He clamped one hand down on the oversize hat as though Grayson might change his mind. "Thanks, mister!" He raced back to his mama, who beamed and mouthed a "thank you."

Deborah waited until they'd moved out of earshot. "That was a nice thing. But you gave him your favorite hat." Her eyes were speculative. "You've never done that before."

He shrugged. "Kid reminded me of EJ."

"Sure it wasn't the boy's name?"

It wasn't often he lied to his mother. But he lied then. "Positive."

Chapter Seven

Stepping off the elevator on her apartment floor, Billie juggled her purse and the bag of groceries with her keys while she listened to her phone messages. She'd spent most of the afternoon pinch-hitting for Elena, who had scheduled three different open houses all at the same time, and the rest of the day trying to save a sales contract for one of her own clients from falling through because of a disagreement over carpet.

It was nearly eight at night. She was tired. Her feet ached. All she wanted was a cool bath, half the package of peanut-butter cookies inside her bag of groceries, and a glass of wine. Not necessarily in that order.

But the sight of Grayson sitting in the hallway with his back against her door made her forget all that. A large paper shopping bag sat on the floor beside him.

She stopped short and had an overwhelming desire to hurry back to the elevator and make her escape.

But he'd already noticed her and was rolling to his feet.

He was dressed in full-on "cowboy" from the snaps on the front of his torso-hugging shirt to the oversize championship belt buckle, drool-inducing blue jeans and gleaming boots. The only thing missing was his trademark black cowboy hat.

She knew he hadn't busted out already in Reno, because one of her voice messages had been from Max as he'd ranted about losing to Grayson by a fraction of a second in their first go-round.

She dropped her phone inside her purse and gave him a sideways look as he shifted so she could put her key in the door lock. "Aren't you supposed to still be in Reno?"

"I have to go back for my second go."

What she really wanted was an answer to what he was doing there outside her apartment, particularly after his abrupt departure the day before. But since she didn't want to ask the question outright, she supposed she deserved what she got.

"Let me help you." He didn't wait for her permission before taking the heavy grocery bag from her.

She turned the key and pushed open the door, going inside. He followed. Again without permission. He set the grocery bag on the counter in her kitchen. "You always work this late?"

"When I need to." She dumped her purse right beside the groceries, before crossing her arms and leaning back against the cupboards.

He still didn't provide an explanation for his presence. Instead, he started removing the items from the grocery bag.

Tall bottle of chardonnay.

Lavender-scented bubble bath.

His gaze roved over her. "Expecting company?"

"Is that so surprising?"

He didn't reply as he turned once more to the grocery bag. Of course she knew what was coming. But short of making a big deal about it, she didn't figure there was anything she could do to stop it.

Out came the giant-sized package of cookies. The small vat of ice cream.

The industrial-sized box of tampons.

"You plan to make a meal on this stuff?"

"Well, not these." She tapped the tampon box, damned if she would be embarrassed. Instead, she picked up the ice cream and stuck it in the freezer, where it could keep company with her ice tray.

He folded up the bag. Without asking, he opened her refrigerator door and plucked out the container of Chinese takeout that sat on the empty shelves alongside a withering orange and two green apples. He opened the container and gave it a wary sniff. "And not that, either." He stuck it back in the fridge. "It occurred to me," he said, as he shut the refrigerator door, "that we sort of had our first fight."

"No," she retorted, before she could stop herself, "you dumped a load of obviously personal information in my lap and then ran." Not to mention running straight to another woman.

His lips compressed. He turned on his heel and left the kitchen. But he returned a moment later with the bag from the hall. "And it occurred to me that I probably owed you an apology." He set the shopping bag on top of the neatly folded grocery bag, pulled out what looked like a boot box, and handed it to her.

"What's this?"

"Open it and see."

She flipped off the lid, half expecting to see a pair of Grayson Gear boots inside.

But she was wrong, and despite herself, she felt a smile start to tug at her lips. She lifted one of the tall rubber muck boots out of the box. "At least you know better than to take me for the glass slipper type."

His expression lightened a little. "I don't know about that." He pulled out another shoebox. This one was cashmere-tan in color, much smaller, and had a very famous name printed on the top.

It was ridiculous the way her mouth went dry as she unsteadily reached for the box. "You didn't really bring me Christian Louboutin shoes."

"I didn't?"

She swallowed and carefully lifted off the top. The patent high-heeled pumps inside were black. Peep toe. Deathly high heel. With the kind of brilliant red sole that she'd seen only in magazines and on Rhonda Dickinson's feet. "You…you shouldn't have." She put the lid back on the box and nudged it with the tip of her finger toward him. "I can't possibly accept them."

"What's the difference between them and the rubber boots?"

"Besides *several* hundred dollars?"

He nudged the box back. "You like shoes."

To be accurate, she loved shoes. But she never spent a fortune on indulging that love, primarily because she ordered all her dress shoes off the internet at a discount site she'd discovered years ago.

Once more, she pushed the box toward him. "They're too expensive. And—" she kept pressure against the box before he could slide it back her way "—how would you even know what size to get?"

"I'm a good guesser."

"I can just imagine how you got good at that."

He lifted one of the ridiculously beautiful shoes out of the box and suddenly crouched in front of her. "Let's test it out."

It was galling to feel a little light-headed, seeing him kneeling that way, and she pressed a steadying hand against the counter beside her. "Grayson, I—" Her words strangled in her throat when he wrapped his long fingers around her bare ankle.

"Lift."

Knowing she ought to resist him was a far cry from being able to do it. She lifted her foot and he slid off the neon-yellow pump she had on.

"You were wearing these the first day we met," he murmured as he set it aside.

"Was I? I, uh, I don't remember." Her lie sounded as strangled as she felt. She swallowed hard and looked away from how his hair waved against the back of his neck. Her fingers curled against the cool granite. But her imagination was conjuring warm skin and thick hair.

He slid the peep-toe creation on to her foot.

Where it fit perfectly.

Then he was rising, and for a moment, his fingertips trailed lightly along the back of her calf, skipping away before he reached her knee.

The damage was done, though. Warmth was flooding through her every nook and cranny.

"Seems like a good fit to me," he murmured. "What d'you think?"

She thought he was standing much too close. She thought that, even with the addition of a five-inch heel, he still towered over her by half a foot. And she thought that he might well be worth her chancing her job. "I think you guessed well." That wasn't her voice, was it? All breathy?

He shifted and the minor distance separating them became nearly minuscule. She could make out every single one of the lashes thickly surrounding his dark eyes. "If you don't accept them—" his voice dropped "—then we've got a problem."

"What problem?"

His gaze roved over her face, seeming to settle on her lips. "I'll have to find another way to apologize." He shifted again and she felt something hard and intrusive nudge against her midriff.

She moistened her lips. "Grayson—" Then some kernel of common sense rescued her. It was the other *shoe* he was holding between them.

What was wrong with her? Had it been *that* long since she'd felt such a visceral attraction to a man?

Yes!

She ignored the answer circling inside her gut and took the shoe as she edged away from him. Feeling almost grief-stricken, she leaned over and slipped the beautiful shoe off her foot. She set it and its mate inside the box and carefully placed the lid back in place. "There's no need for expensive apology shoes because there was no fight."

"Felt like it to me." He waited a beat. "You know, there's nothing going on between me and anyone else."

She couldn't help herself. "Does Bethany Belmont know that?"

"And that's why it felt like a fight." He lifted his hand and she froze when he slid his fingers through her hair, tucking it behind her ear. "She's just an old friend, Billie. We grew up in the same town and both ended up in rodeo. It's nothing more than that."

Her mouth was dry all over again. "This entire conversation is—"

"Necessary?"

"—inappropriate."

"I'll keep it between the two of us, if you will."

She felt like her entire body was buzzing. "Grayson—"

"Is that your phone?"

"What?" Feeling stupid, she looked toward her purse sitting only inches away from her. From inside came a distinct vibrating buzz. She plunged her hand inside and grabbed the cell, silencing it even before she pulled it out to see the screen. Max.

She dropped the phone back into her purse like the hot potato it had become.

"Tell you what. You think about the shoes while we have dinner."

She looked at the wine and the package of cookies.

"While we go *out* and have dinner. There's a new place I've been hearing about and I'm starving."

So was she, but quite probably not in the way he meant. "A *business* dinner." The emphasis was as much for herself as for him.

His gaze roved over her face again. "Sure." There wasn't an ounce of conviction in his response.

God help her. She had no willpower whatsoever.

She jabbed the tip of her finger against his chest. "I mean it, Grayson. I'm going to—" She realized her finger was still pushing against him and quickly pulled her hand away. "I'm going to find some new listings to show you. And we'll review the ones you've already seen. Just in case."

Now, he looked amused. "Whatever makes you sleep at night, darlin'."

If she could sleep at night without dreaming about

him, she would be a whole lot better off. She was weak-willed where he was concerned, clearly, but she wasn't so far out of her mind to admit *that.* "Fine." She started to walk away, only she still had one yellow shoe on and one off. She quickly shoved her toes back into the shoe, where they throbbed and cried a little at the discomfort, particularly now that they'd brushed so briefly against Louboutin heaven. "I'm going to change," she told him.

He held up the tan box. "Don't forget these."

She gave him a look and marched into her bedroom, closing the door.

The bed, made neatly that morning like she did every morning, seemed to stare back at her.

A shiver danced down her spine. Glancing back at the door, she let out a deep breath, giving her bed a stern look as she walked around it and into her closet. She changed out of the blouse and skirt she'd worn all day for work and pulled on a pair of black jeans and a silky purple blouse. She traded the neon-yellow pumps for a more comfortable pair of high wedges and went into the bathroom.

There was too much color in her cheeks, but since nature seemed determined to put it there whenever she was around Grayson there wasn't much she could do about it. She brushed her teeth and brushed her hair. Smoothed on some lip gloss, then tucked her hair behind her ear.

Her fingers froze as she stared at herself in the mirror. She felt Grayson's fingers slipping behind her ear all over again…

And something inside her belly dipped and swayed.

She grabbed the brush again and quickly worked her hair back into a high ponytail, where she could be certain there'd be no need for tucking stray strands behind any ears.

"*Business*, Belinda Marie. Just because flirting is as natural as breathing to him, this is just business. Remember that."

Her reflection nodded back at her and she went out to brave the evening.

All too soon, her intentions went awry. In fact, they didn't even make it out of her parking garage before Billie knew she was swimming in waters too deep for someone who didn't even swim.

Grayson stood beside her car with his hand outstretched.

"You want my keys?" she asked him.

"Yes. I want your keys."

"But nobody drives my car but me."

"One day I'll let you ride Vix. Nobody rides him but me. For tonight, though, *I* want to arrive someplace with you without me sprouting more gray hairs."

She immediately looked at his thick hair. It was a little overlong. And not a single gray that she could see.

He hadn't lowered his hand. "Please?"

It was okay to be accommodating for an important client, she reminded herself. Just not *too* accommodating.

She dropped the keys in his palm. His fingers closed over them, catching her fingers, as well.

"That wasn't so hard, was it?" Still holding her hand, he opened the passenger door for her and didn't release her until she'd slid down into the seat.

The only times she'd sat in the passenger seat of her own car was when she took it to the self-serve car wash and was cleaning out the inside.

He rounded the vehicle and reached down to adjust the power seat before he even tried to sit behind the wheel. When he was in, he adjusted it even more. He fastened his seat belt and started the engine. "Seat belt, Billie."

She shook herself. What was so fascinating about him driving her vehicle? She fastened her own belt and looked through the side window as he drove out of the parking garage.

He cast a sidelong look at her. "You're too young to be such a control freak."

"You try being the baby of a controlling family for a while and see how you turn out."

"What's controlling about your family?"

Her gaze drifted back toward his hand on her steering wheel. "What isn't? I didn't even choose my own college degree."

"You didn't want an economics degree? What would you have chosen instead?"

She crossed her legs against the imagined feel of his fingers drifting up the back of her calf. "It was never an option so I don't even know."

"But you *did* choose to go into real estate."

Right. That had definitely been her own choice. She reached behind the seat and retrieved her phone from her purse and pulled up her Austin Elite app.

"Calling someone?" he asked her.

"Checking for the new listings this week. We can go over them during dinner. What's the name of the place you've been wanting to try?"

"La Viña. It's the restaurant at Mendoza Winery. Been there?"

"Just once. I went to a wedding there not too long ago. The sister of a friend of mine invited me." That was one way to describe Schuyler Fortunado's joyful "the more the merrier" inclusion of everyone working at her father's real estate office, which Maddie now headed. Billie had gone to the wedding only because there hadn't been any tactful way to get out of it.

"Good food?"

"Good food. Good wine." Billie didn't want to think about the wedding bouquet that she'd unintentionally caught when Schuyler's flowers separated midair. Maddie had caught the other part and at the time had said it was a sign. A fact that Billie promptly dismissed where she was concerned. As for Maddie, it had been obvious even then that she and Zach were already head over heels for each other. No magic wedding flowers involved at all.

"The winery is a pretty setting." She was glad her outfit wasn't any more casual than it was, though. "And the restaurant's a popular one. I'm not sure we'll get in without reservations."

She caught his grin.

"Oh. Right. I imagine that's not a detail you have to worry about too often."

He chuckled softly and the sound of it flowed over her like warm honey.

She looked out the window again. Definitely, the waters were way, *way* too deep.

Predictably, when they arrived at the crowded restaurant, the maître d' did a double take when Grayson—after tugging Billie past the people already waiting to be seated—stopped in front of him. He obviously recognized Grayson, though, because he immediately showed them to a cozy table near one of the tall windows reaching from floor to ceiling. "It's a pleasure having you dining with us, sir. My son was one of the participants at the riding clinic you held last year. He still talks about it."

"What's your son's name?"

"Carmelo."

Grayson grinned, nodding. "I remember Carmelo. He was fearless once he got on a horse. Tell him I hope he comes back next year. We're expanding the clinic to include high schoolers and he'd be that age now, right?"

"Yes." The maître d' beamed as he opened the heavy menus and placed them in Billie's and Grayson's hands. "Your waiter tonight will be Alfonse, but please let me know if there is anything I can do to make your evening even more perfect."

"It's mighty perfect already," Grayson drawled, giving Billie a sideways look that made her want to squirm in her seat. "But I appreciate it."

Instead of squirming, she looked around the candlelit tables surrounding them. Even when it wasn't being used as a wedding reception site, the restaurant was unabashedly romantic.

The press of Grayson's thigh alongside hers wasn't helping any. She stared blindly at the menu and tried to focus, and when Alfonse appeared a short while later, she gladly agreed to his suggestion that they ignore the menu altogether and instead enjoy the chef's "special selections."

The waiter moved away again and Billie looked at Grayson. Despite the crowded restaurant, their table still had the feeling of intimacy. "I suppose this happens a lot for you."

"Getting into restaurants without a reservation?"

"That. And the chef's special attention."

She looked up when the maître d' appeared again, this time to introduce them to the sommelier, who proceeded to present them with one of Mendoza Winery's finest. "With our compliments, of course."

With flair, the wine was poured, and once again Billie and Grayson were left alone.

He lifted the long-stemmed wineglass and tilted it toward Billie. "Yeah, and sometimes I'd just like to take out a beautiful woman and be left alone. To peace and quiet and, hopefully, a good steak."

Afraid she'd break the delicate stem of her own glass because her fingers were so shaky, she lifted it toward him in return. "You do know that I'm vegetarian, right?"

Even in the candlelight, he looked surprised. And consternated.

She grinned and sipped the wine, which bloomed against her taste buds as promised. She leaned forward, conspiratorially. "I'm kidding. I'm strictly a 'give me steak or give me death' kind of girl."

He chuckled. "I like to think I'm a live-and-let-live sort of guy, but between the chai tea and no steak, I'd be lying if I didn't say I was relieved."

"Can't have a real estate agent whose palate differs from yours?"

He waited a beat while his eyes captured hers. "Sure."

She stiffened her back against the shiver sliding down it. Sliding into Grayson's appeal would be oh, so easy. And oh, so pleasurable. Until he got bored and moved on. "I didn't know you did riding clinics. Grooming the next crop of rodeo riders?"

"Not quite. We set up the clinics through Grayson Good for kids dealing with various challenges. Physical. Emotional. Financial. Any kind of background. Program's doubled in the last year."

"Here in Austin?"

"All over. About half the towns where I'm rodeoing. I don't even have to twist too many arms anymore to get some of the other guys and gals competing to come on out and help." He smiled wryly. "When we started out five years ago, though, it was a little harder."

"How many kids do you end up with?"

"Depends. It's elementary-school age through junior

high kids, but we kept having to turn away kids once they got too old, so I found another sponsor to kick in so we could go through high schoolers. I suppose we average about fifty to sixty kids at each deal."

She did a little math in her head. "And you remember Carmelo?"

"Might have been harder if he'd been named Jacob. You know how many thirteen-year-old boys are named Jacob?" His lips tilted up as he shook his head.

"Nathan? Is that— Oh." A strikingly beautiful blonde stopped next to their table and propped her hand on a hip that was lovingly outlined by a bandage of a red dress. "You're not Nathan," she said to Grayson, "but you're definitely Billie. Pemberton, if I remember correctly." Schuyler Fortunado Mendoza's vivid gaze bounced from Billie's face to Grayson's and back again. "How the heck are you, sweetie?"

Still bemused as she was by what Grayson had told her, it took a minute before Billie remembered that Schuyler hadn't only married Carlo Mendoza, who was one of the winery founders, but that she worked there, as well. "I'm great, Schuyler. Marriage must agree with you. You look more amazing than ever."

Schuyler grinned. She was even shorter than Billie, but she had a personality as big as Texas. "Marriage suits me *very* well." Her gaze took in Grayson with undisguised curiosity. "So. Let me guess. You're the other brother. The rodeo one."

Grayson returned her smile, though a little less naturally than Billie was used to. "You've got one up on me, I'm afraid," he said.

Right. Billie mentally shook herself. "Schuyler Mendoza, this is Grayson F—Smith. Grayson, Schuyler was the bride at the wedding I mentioned on our way here. Now she's the special events coordinator for the winery."

Schuyler looked pleased that Billie knew that detail, and extended her hand to Grayson. "So nice to meet you, Grayson Fuh-Smith." Her smile widened as she winked. "I've met your brother Nathan, hon. I know all about you Fortune boys."

Billie thought Grayson's expression looked a little doubtful about that, but he shook the bright-eyed blonde's hand without comment.

"How do you like the merlot? We're pretty proud of it, if I do say so myself."

"It's everything that your sommelier promised," he assured her. "Truth is, though, by nature I'm more of a beer kind of guy."

Schuyler laughed. "Sugar, I've heard that your tastes are wide and varied." Her humorous gaze took in Billie as she said it. "Well, you have one of the finest tables in the house and Alfonse is one of our best. He'll take good care of you, I'm sure, so I'll stop intruding on your evening." She bussed Billie's cheek with a quick kiss before sashaying away.

"Good friend of yours?" Grayson asked after they were alone.

"Schuyler's good people. She treats everyone like they're her dear friends. But I really only knew her because I worked with her sister." Billie toyed with her wine stem. "She sure seems to know about you, though." She finally lifted the glass and took a sip. "Fortune boys?"

Grayson grimaced. "I'll have to call Nathan to see what that was all about."

Billie hadn't eaten since that morning and her few sips of wine were already going to her head. Almost as much as he was going to her head. "Being triplets, I imagine you're all pretty close."

"Close enough. I haven't talked to either one of my brothers in a few weeks." His gaze turned to where Schuyler had stopped at another table across the room, where an attractive older couple were seated. "I wonder what her deal is," he murmured.

Billie didn't have to wonder what he was thinking. Schuyler was stunningly beautiful. "She's married," she reminded him.

His dark eyes slid back toward her and he smiled slightly. "And not my type, anyway."

"Not wide and varied enough for you?"

The amusement in his eyes glinted in the flickering candlelight. "My tastes have been narrowing down to more of a fine point lately."

"Well, I hope you're not going to be as picky about real estate as you are about women, or you'll never find your forever home." She couldn't believe the words came out of her mouth.

He let out a bark of laughter.

"It's the wine," Billie muttered, feeling the glances his laughter had drawn their way, and pushing her glass toward the middle of the table. Since the table seemed about the size of a postage stamp, that wasn't very far. "Keep that stuff away."

"I don't know about that. It's helping me get a glimpse into what you're thinking."

She frowned at him. Without her noticing, his arm had gone around the back of her chair and his fingers were flirting with her bare shoulder. "What I'm thinking is that this is supposed to be *business*."

To prove it, she pulled her phone out of her purse and brought up the new listings again. She scrolled through several, dismissing them out of hand because they didn't have any land. When she was finished excluding the unsuitable ones, there were only a few remaining, one of which was the Harmon ranch.

"Here." She set her phone on the table between them so he could see the display. "Three possibles. How much time do you have before you need to be back in Reno? I'm sure I could schedule—"

She broke off when he took her phone and turned it upside down on the table where she couldn't reach it. *"Grayson."*

"Billie."

"You're far too used to getting your own way."

He just smiled slightly and placed her wineglass in her hand. "Indulge me with dinner and I'll look at your listings over dessert."

"You're making that sound like I've invited you to see my 'etchings,'" she grumbled into the wineglass.

He leaned closer until his lips practically brushed her ear. "Is that an offer?"

"Belinda, I thought that was you."

She nearly choked when DeForest Allen stopped next to their table. "Mr. Allen!" She set aside the glass again and it would have tipped right over if not for the smooth way that Grayson caught it. "What a surprise. You, ah, you haven't actually met my client Grayson Smith yet, have you." She quickly made introductions.

"What a surprise, indeed." Her boss's smile looked tight as he shook Grayson's hand. "Anita and I are here celebrating our anniversary."

"Our twenty-fifth." Anita Allen patted her husband's arm. "I insisted on a romantic dinner and DeForest didn't fail me. La Viña is simply wonderful, isn't it?" She leaned closer to their table. "I was going to insist that DeForest take a walk with me in the vineyard, but I just couldn't tear myself away from the excitement." She gave a meaningful little nod toward the table where Schuyler was still talking with the older couple.

Billie had no idea what Mrs. Allen meant, but she was more concerned with the conclusions her husband might be drawing about the cozy picture she and Grayson made, particularly with his arm still around her the way it was. She wiggled her shoulder once, hoping he would take the hint, but he didn't.

"She's just as elegant in person as I thought she'd be." Anita's voice was hushed. She was still looking toward that other table.

"My wife is fascinated by all things royal," Mr. Allen said.

Anita lightly slapped his arm. "Tell me *you're* not impressed that an honest-to-goodness British royal is sitting right over there as normal and natural as you please." She focused on Billie and Grayson again. "I imagine that's Lady Josephine's new fiancé with her. I don't care that nobody really calls her that anymore. She's still a Lady to me. He's a Mendoza, you know. I wonder if they'll have their wedding here? The Mendoza Winery has become *the* place for weddings."

"I don't know about weddings," Grayson said, holding up Billie's phone, "but so far it's been a great place to sit and talk about the ranch I want to buy while we grab a bite. She's been showing me places on her cell." He set the phone down again.

"You're discussing business, then." DeForest didn't look entirely convinced, but his smile was a little less stilted.

"The Harmon ranch is one of the places," Billie added quickly. "So far, Grayson has only seen the exterior."

Her boss's expression cleared and his smile warmed noticeably. Maybe at the thought of the cut he'd be taking if she were to make such a sale. "The Harmon ranch. That is a special property. You'll want to take particular note of the wine cellar—" he gestured toward the wine bottle sitting on their table "—since you obviously have an appreciation." Then he took his wife's arm. "We'll take that walk, dear, and leave these two to their business."

Billie didn't exhale until she saw them walk out of the restaurant. When they had, she reached for her glass of wine and gulped it down.

"You suppose that's the last of our interruptions?"

"I hope so." She set down her empty glass. "Thank you. I believe you just saved my bacon."

Grayson's grin turned wicked. "I have a pretty good appreciation for bacon."

"Don't start," she warned, and flipped up the phone so they could see the display again. "Mr. Allen once canned an agent right on the spot when he was caught playing tonsil hockey with his female client."

Grayson tugged lightly on her ponytail. "We're not playing hockey."

She ignored that. "When *do* you need to be back in Reno?"

He pulled the phone away from her again. "Later." Then he refilled their glasses. The moment he'd drained the last drop, Alfonse whisked the bottle away and replaced it.

"Did you know who she was talking about?" Grayson eventually asked. "Lady Whatsername?"

"Not a clue." Billie picked up her glass. She didn't recognize the slender, silver-haired woman sitting across the restaurant, though she did have a distinctly classy look to her. "If you'd give me my phone back, I could look it up on the internet. Give me five minutes and we'll know all about her."

"Not a chance, darlin'. I'm just a simple rodeo cowboy and I've had more than my fill of internet gossip about me. 'Spect a person like Lady Whatsername has it even worse. Don't feed the beast."

"Simple. Oh yeah, sure."

He settled his arm on the back of her chair once more. "Relax. Drink your wine. The food'll be here soon, and nothing else could possibly go wrong tonight."

Chapter Eight

He was wrong.

Not about the food, which was excellent. As was the second bottle of wine. And the dessert Grayson ordered was mind-bogglingly good. Having him coax her into tasting the chocolate confection right off the tip of his own fork might have contributed to the mind-boggling part, but the restaurant's pastry chef deserved some credit, too.

No. The wrong came about when they actually left the restaurant.

No sooner were they walking out the front door, with Grayson's hand lightly on her waist, than a blinding flash hit them in the face.

Billie instinctively threw up her arm to shield her eyes, belatedly realizing it was a camera flash.

"Whoa, that's Grayson! Almost didn't recognize you without the cowboy hat. Yo, Big G!"

Grayson grabbed her hand and pulled her past the photographer, who'd obviously been camping out in front of the restaurant.

Dizzying strobes followed them. "Who's the new lady? Is she the reason for the five million dollar house you're buying in Austin?"

"Y'all know me better 'n that." Grayson sounded easygoing despite the way he hustled her along the sidewalk toward the parking lot. His stride was so long that she had to jog to keep up. "It's just business."

She heard the photographer laugh. "You gonna take home another win in Vegas this December?"

"You know it, buddy." They'd reached the parking lot, where her car seemed to be parked in the farthest possible slot.

"Just one shot of you and the lady?"

"Only if you promise you're not gonna follow us any farther."

The photographer snickered. "Yeah, sure. Just business, right?"

She felt the sigh work through him, but his smile was pure "Grayson" as he stopped for a few seconds, just long enough for the camera to capture them again. Then the strobe ceased and she blinked against the darkness as she heard the retreating footsteps.

Grayson took her arm again and started walking once more. "Sorry about that."

"You've already bought a five million dollar house?"

"Yeah, that's why I haven't kissed you already. Because I'm working with someone else on a secret real estate deal. You can't listen to stuff like that, Billie. It's all horse pucky."

Her vision was starting to clear. They'd reached her

car. "What do people like that do? Just camp out places hoping to get some little salacious tidbit?"

"Who knows? Maybe he was there for the royal Brit and got a twofer." Grayson unlocked the car and opened the passenger door for her.

One part of her mind wondered if she ought to argue about that, but the more sensible part said she'd had several glasses of wine over the course of the night. "Maybe we should call a taxi. Uber it or something."

He brushed his finger down her nose. "You're the lush. I didn't finish my second glass. In you go, now."

She sank down into the passenger seat. There really was something awfully nice about having someone else take care of things.

Not just someone else.

Him.

When he drove out of the parking lot, she saw bright flashes of lights going off near the restaurant entrance. "Lady Whatsername?"

"Probably. Have you thought more about those shoes?"

"Grayson—"

"Keep thinking." He closed his free hand around hers. "I'm a patient guy."

She let out a short laugh at that. "In what world?"

His teeth flashed in a quick smile.

She leaned her head back. "Where *is* your hat, by the way?" He always wore that black cowboy hat. Except when he'd been in hangover mode, and then it had been a ball cap. But today was the first time she'd seen him without any kind of headgear at all.

"Gave it to a kid wanting an autograph."

She angled her head until she could watch him. "Good thing Grayson Gear sells hats. You probably go through a lot of them if you give them away all the time."

"I don't give 'em away all the time. But this kid was particularly cute. Name was Billy-with-a-*Y*."

Not for a second did she believe the name had prompted his generosity. "I bet you *do* give away a lot of hats."

His lips twitched. "Not my favorite one."

She was suddenly so tired it felt like she was melting into the comfortable seat. "I am going to look up Lady Whatsername," she told him.

"Knock yourself out, sweetheart."

Sweetheart.

If she were in her right mind, she'd never admit how much she liked the sound of that.

Instead, she hugged that secret to herself through the drive back downtown to her apartment building. But when they neared, she made herself stir. Think practically. "I should drop you at your hotel."

"Or...not."

Slippery warmth flowed through her. If she let on how tempted she really was, he'd take that inch and pull her along for a mile. "I should drop you at your hotel," she repeated more or less steadily. "I'll pick you up in the morning."

His smile flashed again as he drove into her parking garage. By the time he parked in her assigned spot, her heart was pounding so hard it was probably visible through her blouse. "I'm...I'm not inviting you up, Grayson."

"Okay." He climbed out of the car and came around to open her door.

"I mean it."

"Okay." He leaned over her just long enough to unclip her seat belt.

But it was long enough for her to inhale the warm

scent of him and her mouth went dry. When he took her hands and gently pulled her out of the car and onto her feet, she was painfully aware that she was on the cusp of letting herself be talked into something that she would ultimately regret. She might be more infatuated with him now than she had been at sixteen, but his business was flirtation. To him, every female walking was *darlin'*.

He closed the car door. Locked it. Then took her elbow and walked with her to the elevator. He pushed the call button. "Give me your hand."

Her legs felt unsteady and she was pretty sure it wasn't the wine. She gave him her hand.

He turned her palm upward and dropped her keys into it. She closed her fingers tightly around them, as if the feel of the jagged edges would help her keep hold of some bit of sanity.

His gaze was steady. "I'll see you after Reno."

It was the last thing she expected him to say. "You're leaving?"

"I've got to catch the red-eye back to Nevada."

She blinked, trying to make sense of it. "You came back just for one evening?"

"I came back just for you."

Her heart skittered around like water on hot oil. "But…but *why*?"

"I told you." He slowly drew his thumb along her jaw. "To apologize."

Her head swam. "You could have done that over the phone."

"I don't particularly like phones."

"Is that why you don't have a cell phone?"

"I have a cell phone. I just rarely use it. Particularly when face-to-face communication is called for." His gaze dropped to her lips and she knew, just knew that once he kissed her, her life was never going to be the same again.

"H-how are you getting to the airport?"

"I'll call a taxi." He smiled faintly. "Or Uber it."

The elevator door slid open.

"Without a phone?"

"I'm a big boy." He gave a quick wink. "I can manage." He nudged her into the waiting elevator, leaned inside and punched the number of her floor. "I'll see you after Reno."

She blinked, watching the doors slowly close. Okay then. The whole kiss thing was her imagination.

But then his hand came up and stopped the doors from closing.

She moistened her lips, her heart charging right back up into her throat.

"Billie?"

"Yes?"

"Think about the shoes." Then he moved his hand away and the elevator doors shut.

She exhaled shakily as the elevator lurched gently and started to climb.

It wasn't the extravagant shoes she was having such a tough time resisting.

It was him.

"Man, it's going to be a helluva week," Max crowed in Billie's ear two days later. "If I do as good in the short round as I just did in my second go, I could walk away from Reno with more 'n ten grand!"

Holding her cell phone to her ear, Billie smiled. She was keeping an eye out for Grayson, who'd arranged—via Deborah—to meet her at her office. It was Sunday afternoon, and even though the Reno rodeo was still going strong until the following weekend, Grayson wasn't waiting that long to see the Harmon ranch.

At least that was the plan. Right now, he was a good twenty minutes late.

She scanned the sidewalks, figuring he'd show up on foot, like he typically did, but there was still no sign of him. And Max was still jabbering away, ninety miles a minute. She waited until he stopped to draw breath. "So where are you heading after Reno?"

"Pecos. Man, I can't wait to see his face when they hand *me* the trophy next weekend. Doesn't matter how good he throws from here on out—it'd take a miracle for him to shave off enough time to beat me on the average! And there ain't anyone else in the lineup who's ever beat my last time on the clock."

She spotted Grayson down the block and felt excitement slide through her veins. He was wearing an off-white cowboy hat. "Who's face?"

"Criminy, Bill. Are you listening or not? I just told you. Grayson's face. He won't be leaving town with his toothpaste-endorsing grin in place when that happens, I can tell you."

"Congratulations. But listen, I've got to run." Grayson had seen her, too, and lifted his long arm in a brief wave as he jaywalked across the empty street, his long, jean-clad legs making short work of it. "I'll talk to you later." She didn't wait for Max's response as she disconnected and pushed her phone into the back pocket of her jeans. Her heart was thumping like mad and she pulled in a deep breath, trying to calm down.

It had been only two days since he'd left her in her parking garage.

Left her in a shaking mess.

He was smiling when he reached her car, and he pulled

down his sunglasses, giving her a once-over. "Nice boots," he drawled.

She looked down at herself. The rubber boots he'd given her reached nearly to her knees. "It's been raining here since you left." She felt oddly shy and half regretted her impulsive decision to wear them. "I'm afraid it might be muddy when we get out to the Harmon ranch."

He looked amused. "Wouldn't want to ruin another pair of high heels."

She moistened her lips and opened the passenger door for him. "Let's get going before someone puts in an offer on the place while we're standing around here on the sidewalk."

The lines beside his eyes crinkled as he pulled off his hat and ducked his head to get into the car. She quickly went around and slid behind the wheel, then started the engine and moved away from the curb. With traffic as light as it was, it wasn't going to take as long as usual to get to the property. "How was your flight?"

"Bumpy." He stretched out his legs. "How's your weekend been going?"

She didn't dare look his way. She'd spent way too much time thinking about him. "Busy. I signed two more new clients yesterday."

He propped his cowboy hat over one knee. "That's great. Congratulations. Good weekend for both of us, then."

She couldn't help glancing at him. "Have you had your second go-round, then?"

"First thing this morning. Got outrode hard by a guy I can hardly stand, but I've still got a chance of making it to the final. Won't know until later this week. More importantly, though, Grayson Good gained another corporate sponsor yesterday to the tune of several thousand dollars."

If he was worried at all about the rodeo, it sure didn't

show. She still couldn't help being concerned that the guy he couldn't stand might be her own cousin. She should have just told him in the beginning. It would have been awkward, but at least it wouldn't feel like a lie the way it did now.

"And now I'm sittin' next to the prettiest girl I've seen all week."

She turned onto the interstate and picked up speed. "I saw the photos last night on the internet of you posing with the rodeo queen, so I'm not falling for *that* line," she said lightly.

He gave her a long look. "Internet, huh? Find out anything interesting?"

She could feel her cheeks reddening. She couldn't tell if he was amused or annoyed. "Merely professional curiosity about a client. I did see a video of your ride there last year. You'd have won if you hadn't had a broken barrier penalty in the final round. Must have been frustrating for you."

At that, he did smile. "It's all part of the ride, sweetheart."

She wished her cousin subscribed to that theory.

While she'd been poking around on the internet, she'd also found out who Lady Whatsername was, but decided to keep that to herself. Lady Josephine Fortune Chesterfield.

For all Billie knew, the woman might be some distant relation of Grayson's. The more she'd read about the Fortune family, the more confusing the connections had become. Particularly when the only detail she knew for certain to be true was what Grayson had told her himself. That Ben Fortune Robinson was his half brother. Gerald Robinson—or Jerome Fortune—was his father. The man whom Grayson said had left his mother high and dry before Grayson and his brothers had been born.

That was pretty much the only nugget of gossip that *hadn't* appeared on her computer screen when she'd made the mistake of following Gerald Robinson's name. The man had founded Robinson Tech and turned it into a household name, but he'd evidently also turned a lot of women into mommies along the way. Women who were not his equally moneyed, society wife, Charlotte. There'd been dozens and dozens of news mentions about his affairs.

Billie's parents might drive her up a tree, but at least they weren't internet fodder like that.

The only complications going on with her family right now were strictly attributed to Billie representing her cousin's competitor and not telling either Max or Grayson.

Her fingers tightened on the steering wheel. She glanced at him from the corner of her eye. "Where's your next rodeo after Reno? Assuming you go back for the short round, I mean."

"I have to go back to Reno even if I don't because there're a few more charity events going on. But the following weekend is Cowboy Country over the Fourth of July. I have to go Red Rock before then, though, to take care of some business. Not sure how many days it'll take. We're not announcing it yet, but I'm close to inking a deal with Castleton Boots to do a line for Grayson Gear."

Her eyes instinctively darted to the cowboy boots he was wearing. She didn't know much about Castleton except they were Texas-based, expensive as all get-out and—according to Rhonda Dickinson, who'd worn them with everything from Daisy Duke shorts to evening gowns—supposedly worth every penny. "That sounds impressive."

"It'll be impressive when we finally come to terms. You ever been to Red Rock?"

"Once. I went to a real estate conference at the Red

Rock Inn. *Trés chic.* I know the real estate market there is healthier than ever these days. Have you been there?"

He smiled lazily. "Honey, I've crisscrossed this state so many times, there aren't many towns I haven't been to. Red Rock's nice. It's no Paseo, though."

She couldn't help but chuckle at that. "Right. Red Rock with its famous ranches and fancy resorts versus Paseo with what? Lots of grass?"

He didn't take offense. "Don't knock all that grass until you try it. Paseo may only have a handful of people calling it home, but that's the way we like it. Won't find Paseo in the news the way you might places like Red Rock or Horseback Hollow, even."

"Didn't you have a tornado in Paseo last year? That made the news."

"Yeah. We were lucky. Didn't have too much damage at the ranch. Nothing major, anyway. That's how Jayden met his wife."

"Wind blew her in?"

He chuckled. "That's more accurate than you know. We all think Paseo is about the most perfect place on earth."

"I'm surprised you chose Austin, then. I know Grayson Gear's office is here, but if you love Paseo so much why make the change?" She was genuinely curious. "Why not move your company to Paseo instead?"

"Be careful before you talk yourself right out of a real estate commission there, sweetheart." He was silent for a while. His long fingers tapped the crown of his hat. "Not a lot of modern technology in Paseo. Keeping a growing business going would be tough. And my twenty-some employees would balk if I asked 'em to leave all that Austin has to offer."

"So it makes more sense for you to come here?"

"Basically."

It wasn't quite the question she'd asked, but they'd arrived at the turnoff for the Harmon ranch, anyway.

The gate was open and she drove through, going slowly to afford Grayson a good look. "I have two more listings to show you after this one."

"Afraid it won't say *home* to me when we walk in the door?"

She sent him a wry smile as she parked near the barn, the same way she had the last time they'd visited the property. "I'll take the fifth on that, if you don't mind."

He gave a bark of laughter and climbed out of the car.

She'd made the excuse about the recent rains to justify wearing the muck boots he'd given her, but she was soon glad for them when he decided to explore outside again before heading to the house. After pulling her foot from yet another sucking hole of mud, she propped her hands on her hips and stared after him. "Grayson, I'm pretty sure we don't need to walk all the way to the lake! Are you just avoiding looking at another house?"

He turned back, gazing at her over the rims of his sunglasses.

She could imagine the sight she made. Mud reaching halfway up her boots. Mud on her butt from when she'd slipped. Mud on her hands from when she'd tried to catch herself. "At this rate, I'm going to have to hose myself off."

"Shouldn't have turned up your pointy little nose when I offered to hold your hand, then." He headed back toward her, grinning. "You could always jump in the shallow end of the pool. I'd make sure you wouldn't drown." He wrapped his hand around her waist, lifting her from the muddy patch as if she weighed no more than a child. "All right, then. Let's get on with it. Walk ahead of me, though, so I can see if you land in quicksand."

He was the quicksand.

When he'd set off on his little walking tour, she *had* avoided the hand he'd offered her. It surely would have been no more disturbing than to have him lift her the way he'd just done.

She rubbed her dirty hands on her jeans, pretending that her entire body wasn't feeling jarred as she picked her way back over the uneven ground. The rain they'd had the day before had cooled the air a few degrees, but she was still grateful for the shade provided by the oak and mesquite trees, even though she cursed the twisted Texas cedar that kept catching the toes of her boots. Fortunately, not all the acreage was so heavily wooded. There was plenty of cleared range just ready for grazing.

By the time they made it back to the outbuildings, her T-shirt clung to her spine and her ponytail to her sweaty neck. On top of the entire mud thing, she was having a hard time maintaining some positivity.

Grayson, on the other hand, just looked damnably sexier than ever. The sheen of sweat on his brown throat. The way he'd rolled up the sleeves of his plaid shirt to his elbows. The only mud drying on him was on the soles of his Castletons and a smear along the bottom of his faded blue jeans.

There were no longer any animals occupying the pens and stalls as they went through the largest of the barns. Primarily, the air was fresh, but there was a distinct undertone that spoke of the days when the pens and stalls had not been empty.

It wasn't unpleasant. Reminded her of when she and Max had spent so many hours hanging around the fairgrounds as teenagers.

She and Grayson passed from the barn back out into

the sun. "Hold up there, sweetheart." He gestured when she glanced at him. "Got a hydrant here."

She turned on her mud-caked heel and joined him where he'd stopped near a tall standpipe sticking out of the ground, topped by a complicated looking spigot. He turned it on and water gushed out. Holding his arm for balance, she stuck one foot, then the other beneath the stream until her boots no longer wore two inches of caked-on mud. Then she washed off her hands and swiped them dry against the back of her T-shirt as she moved out of the splash zone. "Thanks. Water felt good." Almost as good as the pool water had felt the first time they'd been out here.

"Yeah. Hold this." He pushed his cowboy hat into her hand, then ducked his head and pulled his shirt right off over it, buttons fastened and all.

She nearly dropped the hat.

Fortunately, he didn't notice, since he'd basically bent in half so he could sluice water over his head.

Then he straightened, slicking his hair back with his fingers.

She swallowed hard, watching water slide down his roping shoulders and creep along the hard plane of his chest. Then he swiped his hand down to his belt buckle and she swallowed, finally managing to look away. She expected him to pull his shirt back over his head, but he didn't. He just held it bunched in one hand as he took back his hat and settled it once more on his head. "Much better." He waved his shirt in the direction of the house.

She made a strangled sort of sound and started toward it again.

This time, when she opened the lockbox, the house key was there. She opened one side of the hand-carved wood double doors for him, then pulled her feet out of the boots before following him inside. Even though most of the mud was gone, she didn't want to track water inside the house. And at least the boots had done their job; her socks were dry and her jeans from the knees down where they'd been tucked into the boots were cleaner than the rest of her.

He noticed. "Hell. I should take off my own boots."

She shook her head. Heaven help her if he took off even more. "No need. Your boots weren't as bad as mine." She gave him a wide berth as she entered the spacious foyer. Even though she'd studied the listing in preparation, the sheer amount of gleaming hardwood and rough-textured stone was astonishing.

Even Grayson seemed awed. He pulled off his hat and looked up at the exposed beams overhead. "Damn." He dropped his shirt on the foyer table, not seeming to notice when it slipped off the edge and onto the gleaming tile floor.

For the first time since she'd begun showing him properties, she felt a bite of excitement over his reaction.

She plucked his shirt off the floor and set it back on the table, following him silently as he made his way through the house. Unlike most of her clients, who either headed first for the kitchen or the bedrooms, Grayson went for the stairs. Not the grand stacked-stone staircase leading up from the large foyer, either, but the mildly more modest brick staircase leading down from a wide window-lined hall that overlooked the pool.

It was hard not to be sidetracked by all the beauty on display—not the least of which was a shirtless Grayson himself.

But she was supposed to be a professional, so she

made a mental note of a couple obvious flaws. Several cracks in the highly polished Saltillo tile. A faint discoloration in one of the walls that could have come from water damage at one point.

When it came to flaws where Grayson was concerned, there were more than a couple.

A scar beneath his right shoulder blade. Another on his left side, right above his belt. Two more on his ridged abdomen.

They didn't do a darn thing to lessen the overall perfection of him.

It was almost impossible not to gawk at him, but she did her best to focus instead on the house. She followed him blindly through another doorway, and had to stop short just to keep from plowing right into him.

"Suppose the bottles are included with the price tag?"

She looked beyond the bronzed skin three inches from her nose to the wine cellar they'd entered. More stone. More exposed wood beams. And three walls of racks holding what had to be hundreds of wine bottles inset into the brick walls. And in the center of the room a high, thick plank table surrounded by four simple wooden bar stools.

"This is nicer than some wine tasting rooms I've seen," she said.

"Room must have a separate temperature control. It's cooler in here than the rest of the house." His arm brushed against hers as he pulled a bottle from one of the racks. "What d'ya say?" He nodded toward the table. "There's a wine opener lying right there." He gave her a devilish look. "Might be wrong, but nobody'll know but us."

She wagged her finger at him. "I'm onto you, Grayson Fortune. I think there is probably very little that you do that is actually *wrong*."

"Yeah, or I'd have fired you as my agent as soon as I learned about your boss's stupid ethics rule." He reached out and touched her chin, closing her mouth. "Don't look so horrified, Billie. I've been thinking about kissing you since the day we met. But firing you just so that I *could* would be wrong." He slid the wine bottle back into the rack. He picked up the opener and tapped it twice against the wood table. "Besides. I'm a beer guy."

Her heart was racing. "I like beer," she said after a moment. "And, um, and muck boots."

He gave her a long look. "And high-heeled apology shoes?"

She swallowed. She'd obviously lost her mind. But right then, she wasn't sure she cared. "I like those very, very much, too."

With slow deliberation, he placed the wine opener down on the table, and with just as much deliberation, placed his hands on her waist, sending her nerves into a frenzy.

"And if I kissed you?"

She looked at the faint cleft in his chin. At his perfectly molded lips. His deep brown eyes. She couldn't lie to save her life. "I think I'll like that more than apology shoes."

His fingers tightened slightly, drawing her closer. "Not afraid of what your boss would say if he knew?"

She moistened her lips. "Not…not right at the moment."

He smiled slightly as his head lowered toward hers. "When's the last time you kissed someone, Billie?"

"I can't remember," she breathed.

Then his lips met hers. Brushed lightly. Cautiously. Her head still spun and it felt like the earth was falling away. But then she realized he was lifting her onto the table. Bringing her up to his eye level. Her knees just sort of naturally parted to allow him to step even closer.

She wasn't even aware that she'd lifted her hands until she felt his warm, bare skin against her palms. She pressed her fingertips against his chest muscles. "When's the last time you kissed someone?"

"Strange," he whispered back. "I can't remember, either."

Then his mouth lowered again, and this time, there was nothing cautious about it at all.

Sensation grabbed her by the soul and shook her hard. So hard, that when he lifted his head again and lightly rested his forehead against hers as they both caught their breath, she knew that if ever there was a good excuse to get fired, being kissed by Grayson Fortune was it. It was all she could do not to tug him down on top of her right there on the tasting table.

"Well, that seals it," he said huskily. His fingers trailed lightly up and down her spine, sending all manner of shivers dancing through her.

"Seals what?"

"I have to buy this place now."

It took a minute for his words to make sense. But when they did, she planted her palm against his chest and pushed him back a few inches. "What?"

"I'm going to buy this place."

She blinked. "Just like that?"

"Just like that."

"But…but all you've seen of the house is the wine cellar!"

His lips curved. "Doesn't matter. It's my lucky house." He brushed his thumb over her lower lip. "It's where I got to finally kiss you." He dropped another mind-melting kiss on her lips, then pulled her off the table. He didn't seem to care that her legs were almost useless as he nudged her toward the door "Now get on it, sweetheart. Go make the deal!"

Chapter Nine

Thirty minutes later, it was done.

Billie wasn't sure if she felt faint because she'd just negotiated the largest deal of her career, or if it was still the aftereffects of kissing Grayson.

Either way, it didn't really matter.

"Thanks for your time, Bob," she said to the seller's broker. "I'll get the paperwork over to your office as soon as we're back in town."

"Your client's getting a heck of a deal," he said in return. "You ever decide you want to get out from under DeForest Allen's thumb, I'll have a desk waiting for you here at Crenshaw."

She was smiling as she ended the call and went to find Grayson, who'd tired of pacing around the enormous living room while they waited for the seller's response to the offer he'd made.

She found him stretched out on the wide ledge of

the swimming pool. Cowboy hat propped over half of his face. Still shirtless. One arm trailing in the glittering water.

She was still wearing only her socks, so there was no way he could have heard her footsteps as she neared.

But he still moved his hat and swung his feet down as he sat up, his sinewy muscles bulging, his abs rippling. "Well?"

He was everything the good Lord must have intended when designing a man.

She managed to drag her eyes up to his.

"If they're balking because we offered a hundred thousand less than they were asking, tell 'em I'll give 'em full price *and* buy their dang wine to boot." He pushed to his feet.

She shook her head. "They accepted your offer. All we have to do now is get it in writing."

It seemed to take a moment to sink in.

But then he whooped and swung her right off her feet, spinning her around in a circle.

She laughed, caught in his infectious exhilaration. He finally set her back on her feet and grabbed her hand to pull her back into the house. She automatically turned to head for the front foyer, but he had different ideas.

"I want to look at the rest of my house."

She thought of the paperwork that needed to be done as quickly as possible, and dragged her heels. Which, considering they were covered in cotton socks and the floor was covered with slick tile, turned out to be fairly ineffective. "You should have looked while I was on the phone with the owner's broker. A verbal agreement can still go awry, Grayson."

"It won't." He'd pulled her, sliding along the floor, right to the rear staircase that led to the upper floor. "I told you. This is my lucky house. Either pick up your feet, darlin', or I'll pick 'em up for you."

She knew the basement contained the wine cellar, a workout room and another all-purpose room. The main floor had the kitchen, living and dining areas. The upper, the bedrooms.

And after that kiss in the wine cellar, she wasn't sure it was all that wise getting anywhere near a bedroom. The house might be vacant, but it still had enough furnishings so that it showed well to prospective buyers. It was entirely likely there were beds in the bedrooms.

"Grayson—"

"Too late. Seconds are money in my business, sweetheart." He picked her up as if she weighed nothing and tossed her over his shoulder before starting up the stairs.

"Grayson!" Her head bumped against his back and she tried to lever herself up, but his arm was clamped over her backside, keeping her firmly in place. "I'm not a sack of potatoes!"

"I am well aware." He patted her rump.

She couldn't help herself. She giggled. Gave a silent apology to independent women everywhere, then giggled some more and stared down at *his* very fine jean-clad rump.

If her boss were to see her now, he'd be apoplectic and she'd be looking up Bob Crenshaw for a place to hang her real estate license.

Fortunately, DeForest Allen wasn't ever going to know about any of it. At least not before the deal was done. And then she'd have such a whopping commission to her credit it would all be moot.

When they reached the top of the stairs, Grayson pulled her slowly down from his shoulder and she forgot all about giggling. Even though every cell in her body was singing from the contact, she quickly evaded the hands he tried to loop around her waist. "You can look the rest of the house over, but then we really *do* have to get back to my office."

"Your fishbowl, you mean." He hooked her around the waist from behind and kissed the back of her neck.

She shivered and wriggled out of his hold again. "This isn't a rodeo, Grayson. Come on."

"Killjoy," he said, grinning lazily. He waved his hand. "Let's get the thirty-second tour so we can get on to your all-important paperwork."

She gave him a look. "It's *your* paperwork," she reminded him. "I'm not buying a house, two barns, a guest house and a hundred acres. You are."

Grayson's brain still felt rattled from the wine cellar. "Speaking of which. I'd better warn my mother so she can set the money part in motion. She's still in Reno, hanging out with some old friends until I go back." Before he could ask, Billie gave him a knowing look and handed him her cell phone. He placed the quick call as they made their way around the upstairs. There were four bedrooms, each one larger than the last, until the master suite.

Then he stood there in the center of the enormous room, staring out the wall of windows that afforded anyone lying in the bed opposite an unfettered view of rolling hills and pristine lakefront. "Damn. That's a helluva view."

"That's *your* view." Billie padded across the plush carpet and into the en suite bathroom. "Damn."

Her soft exclamation drew him. "What?"

"Three closets." She gestured. "You can pack a lot of pairs of Castletons onto those shelves."

He briefly stuck his head inside the closets, which all led off a bathroom the size of his bedroom back in Paseo, then tapped the toe of his boot against the claw-foot tub situated in a bay of windows. "Nice."

"Wouldn't have taken you for a bath guy."

His imagination didn't need a lot of encouragement when all he had to do was look at Billie to get ideas. She was such a slender thing, they'd both fit in the tub just fine. With only enough space to make things really interesting. "I guess that depends on the company."

Her face flushed. But she didn't look entirely disinterested. He started to reach for her again, but she stiffarmed him, and sidled away. "You've seen the bedrooms. Nothing alarming that makes you want to back out?"

Still smiling, he shook his head. She had no way of knowing he wasn't thinking about the house, at all.

"Okay, then. We have *got* to go." She aimed straight for the stairs and practically skipped down them. She was either afraid to let him get too close or really was in a helluva rush to get to the paperwork end of the real estate deal.

In the foyer, she grabbed his shirt and tossed it at him, and was sitting outside pulling on her rubber boots by the time he joined her. Then she locked the house and stuck the key back in the box.

"What happens to the lockbox now?" With an agreement to his offer to buy the house, he didn't particularly want anyone else having access to the place.

"The seller's agent will pick it up." She started walking toward the car.

It was a toss-up which preoccupied him more. The sight of her denim-covered rear end sashaying ahead of him, or the reality that he was really buying a new home. It was no longer just an idea circling in his head.

Which had him also thinking about the other ideas that had been in his head, too.

He'd just agreed to spend a truckload of hard-earned money. Yeah, he could afford it. But it made a man tend to rethink whether he ought to give up one of the sources of his income or not. Bulldogging was going good. He wanted another championship to his credit, but he didn't *have* to give it all up once he'd achieved it.

They'd reached Billie's car and he looked at her over the roof of it. "What happens after the paperwork?"

"Your earnest money will be deposited in the escrow account while the title company does their thing." She got inside and started up the engine and turned on the AC. "We know the sellers are agreeable to the short escrow you want, and unless something comes up during title or the inspection, you should be able to take possession within a few weeks."

He was the one who'd insisted on the short time frame, so he knew there was no point feeling skittish now. "Middle of next month." After the Cowboy Country Rodeo, he was going to be busy as hell. His rodeo standings were good right now, but that didn't mean he could sit back on his laurels. Not when there were others right on his heels, ready to take his place in the rankings if he gave 'em even half a second. "I won't be able to be around much," he warned her.

"I know," she said calmly. "Cowboy Christmas and all. Don't worry. It'll work out."

He gave her a sidelong look. "What if I need to sign something important and I'm way the hell out in Timbuktu?"

"We *can* do digital signatures these days, you know. All you need is your computer."

He grimaced.

"Oh, what? You don't like computers as well as cell phones?"

"Not much, since I learned the founder of the company that makes both happens to be my old not-so-dear dad."

She lightly touched his hand. "If there is any paperwork that requires your signature, I'll have it messengered to you. Simple enough?"

"Or *you* could bring it." He turned his hand, capturing hers. He ran his thumb over her smooth skin. "Better yet, just come with me."

She gave him a startled look. "Come with you where?"

"Back to Reno. On the road. I'd sort of planned on retiring from bulldogging after this season, but now I'm rethinking it."

She pulled her hand from his, placing it back on the steering wheel. "You're not serious."

"About retiring? Or about having you come with me?"

"Either. Both."

"Never more so. For either. For both." On the other hand, she looked fit to strangle the steering wheel.

"And what would I do?"

He discarded the flippant "me" that was the easy response. "Whatever you like." He offered a grin. "Even on a Robinson Tech device."

"Grayson, I have a job. I can't very well do that if I'm… I'm on the road with you."

Shrugging just then was no harder than it had been six years ago after his final saddle bronc ride, when he'd had to push to his feet from the dirt and wave his hat to a crowd of fifty thousand people even though he'd just cracked two ribs and separated his shoulder. "Yeah, sure. It's not for everyone."

She looked dismayed. "It's not that I don't appreciate the—"

He waved his hand. "Don't worry about it, darlin'. It was just a spur-of-the-moment thought."

She didn't look convinced.

And why would she, when he couldn't remember spewing such bull before?

She was silent for a long moment. "You're still good on buying the ranch, right?"

He barely hesitated. "A deal's a deal."

She smiled slightly. "Okay. Good." Her fingers wrung the steering wheel a few more times. "Great."

He looked out the side window and for once was glad for her lead-foot driving.

The office was empty when they got there. It meant there weren't any lookey-loos watching their every move, but considering everything, he almost wished there had been. At least it would have provided a distraction.

Instead, he paced the hallways while she prepared the paperwork he needed to sign. There were a lot of offices. He wondered if his deal would bump Billie into one of the larger ones.

He wondered if he'd read too much into things. If the universe was finally paying him back for all the times he'd kissed and moved on without a second thought.

He wondered if she'd gone along just for the sake of a freaking real estate deal.

"Grayson?"

He looked away from the office obviously belonging to her boss. She was walking toward him, carrying a thick packet of paper.

Maybe her boss's rule against romantic entanglements wasn't so far off the mark, after all.

"Are you ready to do this?" She held up the pen.

He'd walked into this office with the intention of finding a ranch of his own, he reminded himself. Nothing had changed since then, even though Billie had worked so far beneath his skin he'd let himself forget all his basic rules of life. "That's what I'm here for." He took the pen and walked into the nearest open door—clearly a conference room.

She set the packet down on the long table, explaining each item with painful detail. He wished for some of the speed she saved for her driving. But finally, they got to the part where he needed to sign. And as soon as he did, he handed her back the pen. "Congratulations."

"You're the one who should be congratulated. This is an exciting day for you."

"Finding my *forever* home?" He managed a smile. He could always turn the wine cellar into a trophy room. If he was lucky, maybe a complete remodel would get rid of the memory of kissing her. That wouldn't dissolve the images from their water fight at the pool, though. It wouldn't eradicate the sounds of her laughter, or the intense notion of looking out at that lakefront view from the master bedroom with her lying by his side. "Maybe it'll get you into a bigger office, at least."

"I don't know about that, but it might make up for the Dickinson situation."

"What's the Dickinson situation?"

"It doesn't matter anymore." She toyed with the pen. "Grayson, about your offer…"

He wasn't a teenage kid. He shouldn't feel like everything inside him froze, waiting for her next words. "I told you—"

"I know. Spur-of-the-moment." She moistened her lips. "It's just, well, I'm flattered and…and tempted, frankly. But my job—"

"Tempted." He latched on to the word. "Are you say-

ing that because you were afraid I'd back out of the contract?"

She looked troubled. "No. Of course not."

"You don't even look convinced of it."

"Grayson." She made a frustrated sound and tossed
the pen onto the conference table. It rolled off the other
side. "I've worked really hard to get to this point in my
career. I didn't plan any of this. I don't know if you entirely realize what a whirlwind you are. Walking away
to go on the road with you isn't the kind of decision that
I can make at the drop of your cowboy hat. I've made
commitments here. I have bills and—"

He cupped her shoulders and she broke off, staring up
at him with her pretty brown eyes. "Then put a pin for
now on the road part. After I'm done in Reno, come to
Red Rock with me while I deal with the Castleton folks."
He could see he was making headway and pressed his
advantage. "It's only a couple days. And you can think
about the rest. I've already got a suite reserved at La Casa
Paloma. It's a resort. You've got pools you can dangle
your pretty toes in. Spa treatments. Anything you like.
The suite has two bedrooms. You can lock your bedroom
door if you're worried about your virtue."

Her soft lips parted. "And if it isn't *my* virtue I'm
worried about?"

He leaned down until his lips brushed her earlobe. "If
it weren't for the security cameras around this place, I'd
show you." He straightened again.

Her eyes had darkened. Rosy color rode her cheek-
bones. "I'll think about Red Rock," she said huskily.

He drew his finger along her cheek. "There's a great
Mexican restaurant there called Red. You can wear my
apology shoes."

"I said I would *think* about it!"

Despite the cameras, he leaned down again and brushed his mouth over hers. Not as long as he wanted. Definitely not as deep as he wanted. But it was still enough to leave her breathing unsteadily.

Then he straightened, because they both heard the chime of the front door as someone else entered the office. A second later, her boss came into view through the glass walls.

Grayson went around the table to retrieve the pen.

Then, intent on keeping the progress he'd made from slipping away again because of her boss's untimely arrival, he handed her the pen.

Their fingers brushed.

"I'll be thinking about it, too, Billie," he promised softly. "I'll call you from Reno."

Then he left, giving DeForest Allen a brief nod when they met in the hallway. "She deserves a bigger office," he said without pausing. "Particularly when my Western-wear company starts looking for a new commercial space later this year."

He'd just reached the front door when he heard Billie's exclamation. "Commercial space!"

Smiling, he headed out into the afternoon sun.

"Are you thinking about Red Rock?"

Billie was sitting on the love seat on her terrace, watching the sunset. She cradled the phone against her shoulder and slid down a little until she could prop her bare feet on the table. If she stretched, her toes would brush the cashmere-colored box containing the apology shoes.

"Who is this, now?"

The sound of Grayson's low chuckle made her shiver. "Funny girl."

"Oh, that's right." She curled her toes and the tattoo ring temporarily disappeared. "The guy with the dimple in his chin who doesn't like phones. Whose phone are you borrowing this time?"

"There are still such things as pay phones, sweetheart."

She immediately imagined him standing next to some old phone hanging on the wall, his cowboy hat dipping as he fed coins into it.

"So, are you thinking?"

It had been forty-eight hours since he'd left her office. Forty-eight hours of thinking about him. About Red Rock. About the fact that—wise or not—she wanted to go with him and she had no intention of locking her bedroom door when she did. "Yes, I'm thinking."

"So am I." His deep voice dropped even deeper. "Want to know about what?"

He was over a thousand miles away, but he might as well have been sitting right next to her. Every cell in her body hummed. "How about I tell you how your escrow is progressing?"

"Some might consider that a buzzkill."

She smiled into the sunset. Her terrace was peaceful, but in Grayson's background, she could hear music on the loudspeakers and the rodeo announcer's voice. "Some might. I've scheduled the inspection for tomorrow."

"Thrilling."

"It will be once you know you won't be looking at replacing a roof the second you move in, or dealing with a foundation leak or something just as bad."

"It's my lucky house. Everything is going to be fine. Don't be a worrywart."

"It's my job to be a worrywart on behalf of my clients. Particularly ones who were ready to plunk down a fortune on a property as is. And you know, you really threw my boss into a tizzy with that line about Grayson Gear needing new space. It's all he's talked about for two days."

"We do need new space. Ask my manager, Jess. She's been harping on it for over a year."

"I haven't done a lot of commercial real estate. You'd be better off with one of our associates who has."

"I don't want one of your associates. I want *you*."

Her stomach swooped, taking the words in an entirely intimate way. Her brain, however, was determined to stay the course. "I wouldn't want my inexperience to adversely affect your company."

"You don't want the business?"

"Well, of course I want it. But—"

"If anyone else but me dangled that in front of you, would you hesitate?"

She couldn't help but smile wryly. "No."

"Well, then, sweetheart, buck up. One of the first things I liked about you was that you've got grit."

"Oh. Flattering. Compare me to John Wayne, why don't you."

"John Wayne doesn't turn me on like the thought of you going all 'real estate' on me." He waited a beat. "What're you wearing?"

She had to take a second to catch her breath. But two could play that game. "Maybe I'm lying in my bathtub, surrounded only by bubbles."

"Ah, sweetheart," he drawled. "You're killing me. But I'll bet you're really sitting on your patio wearing cutoffs and a Rice T-shirt, with a bottle of wine and a package of cookies on the table in front of you."

She laughed softly. The wine was there. As yet unopened because he'd called her before she had a chance to use the corkscrew. But a pair of outrageously expensive shoes replaced the cookies of his version.

It was silly that she'd brought the shoebox out and set it on her coffee table. The truth was, though, that she'd been keeping the box close by no matter where she was in her apartment. And it wasn't so much the shoes themselves, but more what they represented.

Or maybe even *who* they represented.

No matter how tempting, the shoes inside the box felt unattainable.

The same thing could be said of Grayson.

Despite his persistent pursuit, she was afraid to let herself believe anything long-term would come out of it.

"I'm right, aren't I? See how well we've gotten to know each other?"

"Let's just say you're close." She decided it was safer not to tell him that the cutoffs and T-shirt were in the dirty laundry, so she was wrapped in a silky robe that didn't do a darned thing to soothe her hypersensitive nerves.

She stretched out her foot a little farther and nudged the lid off the shoebox. The red soles inside beckoned. She leaned forward, intending to grab the wine bottle and opener. Instead, her fingers drifted to the shoes. And it was a foregone conclusion that they'd end up on her feet from there.

Propping her high-heeled feet up on the table, she eyed them and sighed a little. It was much too easy remembering the feel of Grayson's long fingers on her ankles when he'd slid them on to her feet.

"Now what're you doing?"

A hot flush ran under her skin. She quickly slid the shoes off again, tucking them safely right back into the box. "Nothing."

She could practically hear the slow smile on his face. "You're wearing the shoes."

Her bare toes pushed the box a few inches away as if he could see her. "No, I'm not."

"You might as well accept it, sweetheart. Those shoes are meant for you."

Like he was meant for her?

She tried to banish the fruitless thought, but it wouldn't go. "They're too extravagant and I *will* be returning them to you. So accept it. *Sweetheart*."

"Aww. That's your first 'sweetheart.' You're making my heart go all pitter-pat."

She laughed. "You're nuts."

"Well, I could get serious and promise that one day, you'll wear those shoes and nothing else while we make love." He paused, making her wonder if he could hear the sound of her pounding heart right through the phone line. "But…I wouldn't want to scare you off. Not when you're supposed to be thinking about Red Rock."

Her head fell back against the cushion. "You're relentless."

"When there's something I want? That's what has got me where I am today, sweetheart."

"In Reno. A thousand miles away."

"Closer to two. It's only a plane ride, Billie." He sounded serious. "Say the word. And I'll get you here in a matter of hours."

Word.

She closed her eyes. "The inspection is tomorrow. And after that, I have to go to Houston."

"What's in Houston?"

"The rest of my furniture."

"So you *do* have more than boxes?"

She smiled. "I have a couch, even. It's been stored

in my old neighbors' garage. But they're moving into a house soon that I helped them find, so one of my brothers, Ted—he has a pickup—is going with me to get the last of my stuff. It won't take us long. What about you? Will you have a lot of stuff to move to your new place?"

"I've got my horses, my gear and my bedroll."

"Sounds like you'll be doing some furniture shopping, then."

"Maybe for a bed." His voice dropped a notch. "It'll go against the wall where it'll overlook the lake. What do you think?"

"I think we should talk about something else."

He laughed softly.

She cleared her throat. "Why are you reconsidering retiring? Why were you even considering it in the first place?"

"*That's* what you want to talk about?"

It was a safer subject than her future, which seemed so much less certain than it had just a few weeks ago... before he'd walked into her office. "I've got you on the phone," she said lightly. "I figure I'd better take advantage of it."

"I'm thirty-seven, Billie. Bulldogging's hard work."

"There've been successful steer wrestlers older than you."

"And there've been unsuccessful ones, too. I've been thinking about it for a long time. If I'm gonna quit, I want to quit on top."

"On your terms." Ego, she understood. "When did you start reconsidering?"

"When I found myself buying a ranch twice as big as I'd figured I'd want."

All because he'd kissed her in a wine cellar. As romantic gestures went, it was a pretty huge one. "You need the money. If you've changed your mind about buying the ranch, better to do it now, rather than later."

"I *want* the money. No offense, Billie, but you of all people should understand that. You told me yourself you chose your career because of the income potential."

She'd told him she was tired of hand-me-downs. But the bottom line was the same. She wanted—needed— to be self-sufficient. Trotting after him on the rodeo circuit flew right in the face of every goal she'd ever had. "What you're spending on the ranch will take more than a few years at the top of the money rankings to recoup, won't it?"

"It's not the rodeo money. It's the endorsement deals I have as a result. Billie, I can afford the ranch. I could afford two of 'em and not really sweat it. But I spent more of my life *not* having money than having it. So it's kind of second nature for me to hold on to it when I can."

Except when he was donating small fortunes to help fund the work that his foundation did.

"You're an interesting man, Grayson Fortune."

"Well, hell, Billie. Next thing you'll be saying is that I'm a good friend."

She smiled slightly. "From your tone, I take it that is bad."

"It is when it's coming from the girl I'm tryin' to woo."

Her smile widened. "I've never been wooed before."

"Not even by the guy who inspired the toe tattoo?"

She wriggled her toes. "Not even by him."

"Does it earn me any points?"

She stared out at the glorious sunset. Imagined the same view from a lakefront bedroom with him by her side. "You're sure not losing any."

Chapter Ten

"You know he got her freaking pregnant, right?"

Billie nearly jumped out of her skin at the sound of the furious voice. "Max! I thought you were still in Reno!"

Her cousin stepped into her office cubicle and planted his hands on her desk, leaning toward her. "Did you hear what I said?"

She looked nervously at the glass walls surrounding her. It was Wednesday afternoon and the office was hopping. "Keep your voice down. There are people here trying to conduct business." She pushed him toward her side chairs. "Sit down."

He didn't budge. "How could you, Bill?"

"Who is pregnant? And what do *I* have to do with it?"

"He'll just use you, same as he did her. And then he'll throw you away, same as he did her."

"What are you talking about?" But her stomach was already sinking.

"Who do you think? Your new boyfriend, Grayson the Great. What the hell, Billie? Did you forget what loyalty to your family was all about?"

She hopped up from her chair and it rolled back, knocking noisily into her filing cabinet. "Keep your voice down!" She grabbed his arm and hauled him down the hall and into one of the conference rooms. It was surrounded by glass, too, but full walls of it that afforded a fair measure of soundproofing. She pushed the door closed and looked at him. "Grayson's a client." It was the understatement of the year. "And how'd you even hear about that?"

He shoved back his cowboy hat. "Are you kidding me?"

She frowned at him. "Did Grayson tell you?" They were both competing at the rodeo in Reno. She still hadn't given Grayson any reason to connect her with Max, but she had no idea what kind of conversations went on between men when they were hanging around waiting to wrestle an enormous animal to the ground.

"Like I'd listen to anything *he* said." Max's voice was filled with disgust. He'd pulled out his cell phone and was fiddling with it. "There." He flipped the phone between his fingers so she could see and hear the video playing on the screen.

"Is she the reason for the five million dollar house you're buying in Austin?"

"Y'all know me better 'n that. It's just business."

With a swipe of his finger, Max silenced Grayson's words. "Two of you didn't look like you were doing much *business.*"

It was from the night they'd been to La Viña. It seemed so long ago, but had really been less than a week. "Where did you find that?"

"I didn't have to find it. It's all over the news that

he's buying that big ol' Southfork-sized ranch outside of town." He made a face. "'Is Grayson finally settling down?' That's the question the media keep asking. Geez, Billie, I knew you were still crushin' on him. I can't believe you worked with the guy after what you know about him!"

"I had a job to do, Max. It's not like I can afford to pick and choose who my clients are!"

He waved his phone in her face. "And you can't choose who you're hitting up the latest hot spot in Austin with?"

"It was a business dinner," she said through her teeth. *The business of you falling for Grayson, maybe.* "Look, Max. I'm sorry if you think I've betrayed you, but none of this was about you!"

His look turned pitying. "You still don't get it. She. Is. Pregnant."

"She *who?*" Even as the exasperated words burst from her, she realized the answer. "Bethany."

"Bethany." Max rubbed his hand over his face.

But she still saw the gleam of moisture in his eyes and her shoulders suddenly fell.

This was the boy she'd grown up with. The one who was more a brother than a cousin.

"Oh, Max," she breathed. "You really loved her."

He dropped his hand, glaring at her. "I told you I did. You think I made it up?"

"No, but…" She spread her palms. "You've never been serious before about anyone and I thought—we all thought—it was just another fling."

His jaw worked. He grabbed a chair several spaces down the table and sat in it. "It's his, you know. The baby."

Her stomach clenched. "Grayson's not involved with Bethany. They're just old friends. He told me."

"And you believed him, Little Miss Don't-Believe-in-Love." He snapped his fingers. "Just like that." He leaned forward. "He gave her a job. He gave her money."

Billie didn't want to believe it. "How do you know that?" She couldn't imagine Max actually talking to Grayson about it. Not the way he felt. "Did Bethany tell you?"

His lips twisted. He looked away. "She won't see me."

"Then how—"

"Heard it from his hazer." He made an impatient sound. "Lou Blackhorn. He's Grayson's regular hazer and he's been filling in for Trav for me in Reno."

"This Lou…he told you specifically that Grayson paid Bethany money because she's pregnant with his child." Saying the words made Billie more than a little nauseated.

"No, he didn't tell me specifically, but I heard it all the same. Your boyfriend got her knocked up and now he's moved on to you." He pointed his finger at her.

She shook her head. "You're wrong."

"He's not trying to get into your pants?"

She flinched. "Don't be crude."

Max snorted. "Right." He shoved out of the chair. "Well, next time he does, just remember what I said. He'll use you, same as he used her. And when he's finished, he'll move on to the next and the next and the next." He yanked open the conference room door and stormed down the hall out of sight.

She exhaled shakily, lowering her forehead onto her hands while Max's words rang inside her mind.

"Billie?" A tentative voice interrupted her misery. She looked up to see Amberleigh's concerned face. "Are you all right, hon?"

She lowered her hands to her lap and nodded. "I'm fine, Amberleigh. Just…just family…stuff."

The older woman nodded sympathetically. "Your two-o'clocks are here to sign papers. I came to find you when you didn't answer your line. I can see if someone else can handle it. Elena's in this afternoon, I think—"

"That's okay, Amberleigh." Billie pushed to her feet. "The Nguyens are my clients." Lana Nguyen was also the secretary of Ben Fortune Robinson that she'd mentioned to Grayson.

The same day he'd told her Robinson was his half brother.

"I was just printing out the rest of their paperwork when I got interrupted," she said around her tight throat. "I'll be there in a minute."

"Okay." Amberleigh gave her an encouraging nod. "Family stuff works out, hon. Don't forget that."

Billie smiled sadly. She was sorry that Max was hurt, but she knew that eventually, everything between them *would* work out.

Grayson, however, was another situation entirely.

Why on earth had she ever let herself believe that he would be different? That he was worth risking her entire future on?

He was Grayson Fortune. Flirtation was his stock-in-trade.

Amberleigh's gaze dropped to Billie's feet before she started walking away. "Meanwhile, those are some pretty spectacular shoes. They ought to make everything feel better. Are they real?"

Billie looked down at the red-soled pumps. "They're real," she murmured. She followed the receptionist out of the conference room. "But they're going back."

She just had to figure out the proper way to do it.

* * *

"Just another picture, folks. Grayson, why don't you put your arm around our rodeo queen here?"

It was the same routine he'd followed at hundreds of rodeos. Holding the championship spurs in one hand. Dropping his other arm around a beaming rodeo queen. He'd even done it more than once right there in Reno.

Only difference this time was that Billie was here.

He'd spotted her beyond the glare of the grandstand lights. She hadn't made any move to approach him yet from where she stood off in the shadows, but he'd still recognized her. She wore jeans and a short jacket—not much different than a lot of women there—but he would recognize the shape of her anywhere.

"That's great now, folks. Grayson, how about—"

He lifted his hand, cutting off the photographer. "Sorry." They'd already gotten plenty of pictures. "Have someone I need to see." He tipped his hat to the rodeo queen and headed off to Billie. Anticipation made short work of the walk across the arena.

Until she stepped out of the shadows and he saw the shoebox she was holding.

The leap inside him didn't fully nosedive, though, until he saw the unsmiling look on her face.

He closed the rest of the distance. Ignoring the shoebox, he reached for her shoulders, dropping a kiss on her cool cheek despite the stiffness he felt in her. "This is a surprise. When did you get here?"

"In time to see you win the final round. Everyone thought the numbers were against you, but you surprised them all."

He'd surprised himself, too. Breaking his own fastest time. Setting another record. "If you'd have told me you were coming, I would have made arrangements—"

She shook her head before he could even finish. "I didn't plan at first to come." She looked away. "But I couldn't just send these by messenger, either." She held out the box.

There was no question that it contained the red-soled apology shoes. He didn't take it. "Those were a gift."

"I told you I couldn't accept them. And now…" Her lips twisted. She shook her head again and her sleek hair slid down over her cheek.

"And now…what?"

"Yo, Big G. Sweet run, man." A man in clown makeup brushed past them as he jogged into the arena, where two women on horseback were circling the arena with flags, preparing the boisterous crowd for the next event while rock music blasted from the loudspeakers.

The interruption had been brief, but Billie had still backed away from him even more.

He stifled an oath and closed the distance again. "Let's go somewhere more private."

"It's really not necessary." She sidled away again, holding out the shoebox.

"It damn sure is if you think I'm going to let you shoe and run without at least tellin' me why first." He took her elbow, and steered her around a bunch of giggling teenage girls carrying sodas and cotton candy.

"Hi, Grayson," they chimed like a chorus.

He tipped his hat. "Ladies." But he didn't slow his steps. Nor did he release Billie's elbow, despite her effort to pull free. He aimed away from the lights and the crowds, bypassing the animal pens and heading for where his own trailer was parked out on the dirt. The people they were likely to encounter here were more interested in loading up their horses and their gear and pulling out for the next stop than they were with Grayson and Billie.

"All right." When he reached the side of his horse trailer, he turned to face her. "What bee have you got in your bonnet? Last time you and I talked, you were all but set to go to Red Rock with me."

Her jaw worked from one side to the other.

"Dammit, Billie!" He grabbed the shoebox and tossed it onto the open tailgate of his pickup. "Just talk to me."

Without the box to clutch to her waist, she folded her arms tightly over her chest. "I know about the baby, okay? I know!"

He stared hard. It was nearly dark and there were more shadows than there was light shining from the lampposts. "What baby?"

"*Your* baby!"

He felt a jolt deep inside his gut. No matter how randy his past was, he'd always been damn careful. Considering his upbringing, he knew better than to carelessly make a baby that way. "If I had a baby, I think I'd know about it, darlin'."

"There's no reason to hide it. Max told me. You and Bethany—"

"Max." His brain felt sluggish, trying to keep up. "Max Vargas?" He knew Bethany had briefly dangled the younger man from her strings. "How—"

"Max is my cousin." She cupped her elbows, looking miserable.

Whether she was as miserable as he felt seemed debatable at that point. "Your cousin." He waited a beat. "And you're just now thinking to mention it."

"I didn't think it was relevant—"

"Relevant." He'd told her about Jerome Fortune/Gerald Robinson being his father. But she couldn't mention that the guy who'd been dogging his heels for months was her cousin. Grayson resettled his hat, trying to contain his temper. It wasn't often that he lost it, but he knew he was as close to that line as he'd ever been. "When did you think it *might* get relevant?"

"It doesn't matter anymore."

"The hell it doesn't."

"Grayson? Everything all right here?"

Billie startled even more than he did at the sound of his mom's voice. He hadn't heard her approach.

His jaw felt so tight it was hard to speak. "Yeah." He looked from his mom to Billie. "You remember—" Billie, he'd been about to say. But he was too damn mad. Instead he added, "—my real estate agent?"

Deborah smiled, though he could see the concern behind it. "Of course. Billie and I have talked many times since we first met."

"She's Vargas's cousin," he said abruptly.

Deborah's eyebrows rose a little, but she didn't seem to be anywhere near as annoyed about it as he was. "I've always thought it was a small world. Grayson didn't mention that you'd be here. Is everything coming along with the ranch contract?"

Billie tucked her hair behind her ear. She didn't look at him. "Yes, it's progressing just fine."

"Good to hear." His mom gave Grayson a searching look. "Do you want me to start loading up Vix and Van?"

He shook his head. "I'll get to it in a few."

"Well, I'll leave the two of you to it, then." Deborah started walking away.

"I'm not staying," Billie said quickly. She started edging back.

He blocked her path. "You're damn sure not going," he said in a low voice. "Not without explaining yourself."

"Explaining *myself*?" Her gaze darted to his. "What about you and Bethany?"

"I told you we were old friends." He grabbed her arm. "Wait. You think her baby is mine. Because your cousin Max spewed a load of BS about it."

Billie's chin came up. "You deny giving her money?"

"No, and that doesn't mean a damn thing. Neither does my giving her a job at Grayson Gear. She's not pregnant with my kid. If she were, I'd be the first one to tell you. Not Max." He spread his arms. "You know what? You're right. There is no reason for you to stay. From the start, I've been an open book with you. Instead of just telling me the truth about your cousin, though, you'd rather believe whatever line he's feeding you. You want to think the worst of me, you go right on ahead, darlin'. Frankly, I'm too old for that crap."

Even in the thin light, he could see the sheen in her eyes and steeled himself against it.

"Don't worry, though. Your precious real estate deal is still safe. You'll earn your sales commission."

She winced. "I'm not worried about the commission."

"Then why didn't you just tell me about Max?"

"Because at first it wasn't important! You were a brand-new client and that's all." She visibly swallowed. "And by the time it was important," she said in a lower, raw-sounding tone, "I didn't know how."

"What's so tough? 'Hey, Gray. Funny coincidence. One of the guys gunning to dethrone you is my cousin.'"

"Easy for you to say now!" She looked away, folding her arms again.

"You could've trusted me."

Her jaw worked. "We hardly knew each other."

"Bull."

"It hasn't even been a month since we met!"

"I don't care if it's been a week or a year." He pointed at her. "You're the cynic. Expecting the worst when it comes to anything but work. Bethany's baby isn't mine," he said flatly. Clearly. "For the simple reason that I never slept with her. Not even back in the day when I was trying to do exactly that. So next time you talk to your cousin, maybe you can suggest he stop tossing blame around when he oughta be looking in his own backyard."

"You think the baby could be *his*?"

"I don't know. At this particular moment in time, I don't much care. That's their deal." Grayson waved his hand between her nose and his chest. "This, though? The fact that your first reaction is to think the worst about me? That's our deal. Which, as far as I'm concerned, means there is no deal." He reached around her and grabbed the shoebox. "You might as well take 'em, darlin'. They don't mean jack to me." He pushed the box into her hands and turned away.

"Grayson." Her voice sounded thick. "For what it's worth, I *am* sorry."

His steps barely hesitated. "So am I, Billie." Pushing the words out was a helluva lot harder than it should have been. "So am I."

"Anything you want to talk about, son?"

"No." Ignoring his mother, Grayson kept guiding Van into the trailer, where he'd already loaded up Vix. When he'd walked away from Billie to get the horses, he'd known she wouldn't be there when he returned more than an hour later.

And he'd been right.

Considering her anxiousness to leave, she'd probably turned tail and bolted the second he'd disappeared from view.

Knowing he'd told her to go didn't make up any for the sting of knowing she hadn't cared enough to stick around and fight for them.

"You sure?" His mother held up a red-soled shoe.

Even though Billie had left, she *still* hadn't taken the damn shoes.

"I don't want to talk about it."

It was either that or succumb to the urge to punch his fist through the side of the trailer. Which he couldn't do for several reasons.

One, he'd end up breaking his hand.

Two, he'd up having to answer even more questions from his mom.

He ran his palm over Van, needlessly checking the wraps on the horse's legs.

"Grayson."

"I don't want to talk about it, Ma."

"I know those are the shoes you bought for Billie."

That's what he got for having his personal manager write most of the checks to pay his bills. "I said I don't want to talk about it." He'd never once had a woman refuse a gift.

But then he'd never once bought a woman infernal apology shoes, either. Or gotten involved with someone determined to have so little faith in him. Or gotten involved, period.

He climbed out of the trailer again to where his mother was standing. "Throw the shoes away. Give 'em away. Either way, I don't care."

"Grayson, you don't mean that."

"The hell I don't." He closed the trailer doors and secured them. "I want to get on the road. It's a long haul to Red Rock." Made even longer by the fact that he was pulling a trailer and two horses that periodically needed a decent break from the ride.

They took care of him in the arena. It was up to him to take care of them outside of it.

Deborah tucked the shoe back into the box with its mate. "Maybe I should go with you."

"Why?" They'd already made the travel plans. She was flying back to Texas in the morning, with the intention of spending a few days in Paseo before meeting him in Horseback Hollow for the rodeo next weekend.

"Because you're obviously upset. Clearly, Billie is special to you."

"Might be time for a vision check." He dropped a kiss on his mom's forehead just to reassure her. "I'm pissed off, but I'm not gonna drive a fortune in horseflesh and equipment off the road because of it."

"But—"

"Ma, enough."

She exhaled noisily. "It's not a sin to admit you're hurt, Grayson. I'm not so old that I don't remember how it feels."

"You'll never be old." He started walking around the trailer, automatically checking every latch.

Deborah's voice followed him. "If you think that's flattering enough to distract me, you're wrong."

He ignored that. She was standing right where she'd been when he made it around the trailer. "You going to be okay getting from the hotel to the airport in the morning?"

She made a face. "Strangely enough, I think I will be." She was having a late dinner with a group of rodeo sponsors, and she had her own rental car. "Don't worry about me. Worry about what's going on between you and Billie."

"Nothing's going on. Not anymore." His lips twisted. "If it ever had a chance, her habit of thinking the worst took care of it." He shot his mom a look. "And I am *not* talking about it."

"I don't know whose stubbornness you inherited more of. Mine or your—"

He raised his palm. "Don't even say it."

"Well, unsaid or not, it's still true. If either one of us had been less stubborn, who knows what might have happened."

God help him. At least with hours on the road ahead of him, he wouldn't have to listen to anyone or anything but his own thoughts.

And those he could drown out thanks to the miracle that was satellite radio.

Chapter Eleven

"You're dating Grayson?"

"Can I meet him?"

"Why haven't you been returning my calls?"

Billie had barely arrived at her parents' annual Fourth of July barbecue when the questions started accosting her.

"Happy Fourth," she said in return as she placed the tray of brownies she'd brought onto the table set up in the grass near the back door.

"Belinda Marie!"

She ignored her mother for the moment and bypassed the inflatable kiddie pool filled with teenagers as well as kiddies, then weaved around the others sprawled in lawn chairs near the television that had been dragged outside, and finally made it to her father, where he was tending the meat sizzling on the grill. She kissed him on the cheek. "Hi, Daddy. What you got cooking there?"

He waved his long-handled tongs. "Usual ribs and chicken. How's work?"

She thought about the check that she'd received the day before. The check that was still sitting in her purse.

The sale on the Harmon ranch had gone through in record time. And the payment was her share of the commission.

"Closed on a property just yesterday."

"Get enough commission to pay your rent?" He winked through the barbecue smoke swirling around him.

"A few months." It was a wild understatement. Hands down, it was her largest commission yet. But she'd never been less excited about a sale closing since she'd first gotten her real estate license. Even the new, larger office that Mr. Allen had assigned to her hadn't generated any feeling of accomplishment.

"Good for you, baby. Run and get me another beer, would you?"

"Sure." She headed for the insulated cooler that was sitting in the shade of a tree, where her eldest brother was stretched out on a lounger. As she bent over the cooler, she could see the television screen several feet away. From experience, she knew the channel wouldn't stay the same for long. Between the Cowboy Country rodeo, baseball and NASCAR, there were a lot of things they'd be watching.

She looked the other way and plunged her hand into the ice and water filling the cooler. She had no intention of even inadvertently catching any of the rodeo.

"Hey, peanut." Her brother barely moved the cowboy hat covering half his face. "What's the deal with the rodeo king?"

"Not you, too, Ray."

He lifted his hat far enough that he could give her a

stern look. "I'm not sure I like the idea of you sleeping with that guy. He's got quite a reputation."

"According to who? Max?" She pointed her finger at her brother. "First, I'm not sleeping with him, but even if I were, it's none of your business."

"You're my baby sister. That makes it my business."

She gave him a look. "Interesting, when you've never seemed to care in the least who I might have been sleeping with before now."

He looked pained. "My ears! You're too young to be sleeping with anyone. Especially a walkaway Joe like Grayson. He's a rodeo rider, peanut. And to hear Max tell it—"

She raised her hand. "Max is misinformed." She would regret to her dying day assuming Max was correct about Bethany's pregnancy, even though it didn't change anything. "Grayson's also a business owner and a philanthropist, in case you're interested in the facts. None of which matters because I'm *not* involved with him!"

Her voice rang out in the sudden silence that just naturally had to fall right then.

She looked at the expectant faces around her.

She focused first on Selena. "I'm sorry, sweetheart. But I don't think I'll be able to introduce you to Grayson. My business with him is done." And after the things they'd said in Reno, she had no expectation of seeing him again now that the real estate deal was concluded.

She hadn't even been present at the closing, as was her usual practice. Instead, the final paperwork had been handled two days ago, entirely in Horseback Hollow, where he was staying for the three-day rodeo.

Selena looked disappointed. "I tried to get Mom and Dad to go to Cowboy Country for the rodeo finals today, but they didn't want to drive that far for just a day 'cause it's too expensive. And I couldn't just go with Aunt Mae and Uncle Larry, 'cause I'd a' had to miss school. Otherwise Max could have introduced us." She waved at the television. "We're stuck watching it on TV."

Billie smiled sadly. "I don't think an introduction would have happened, even if you had found some way to be at the rodeo. Max and Grayson don't exactly get along."

"Why not?"

She exhaled. How much could she explain to a thirteen-year-old?

"'Cause Max wants to be better than Grayson," Peggy said tartly as she joined them. She plucked the forgotten beer out of Billie's hand and stuck it back in the cooler, pulling out a bottled water instead. "Take that to your uncle Hal," she said, handing the water to Selena. Then she wrapped her no-nonsense hand around Billie's arm.

"I don't appreciate you ignoring my phone calls." Her mom pulled her toward the house.

"I wasn't ignoring them." It was an outright lie. "I've just been busy with work."

"Pfft," Peggy said dismissively. She hauled Billie into the oppressively hot kitchen and crossed her arms. "Well?"

"Well what?"

"Don't take that tone with me, Belinda Marie."

Exasperated and miserable, Billie threw out her arms. "What do you want me to say, Mom? Grayson was a client."

"That's all? That's not what the news people have been saying."

She opened her mouth to deny it, but the words wouldn't come.

She swallowed and looked away. "Nothing they're saying in the so-called news is accurate except that Grayson was buying a ranch. It doesn't matter now, though. He thinks I don't trust him because I didn't tell him about Max, and Max hates me because I didn't tell him about Grayson."

"Because of that Bethany Belmont business?" Peggy's lips compressed. "Mae told me everything."

"From her son's viewpoint, I'm sure," Billie muttered.

"Max is always quick to overreact."

"He's really hurt this time. He cares more about her than we thought."

"And are you hurt?"

"That Max is mad at me?"

Her mom gave her a look. "Over Grayson."

"It doesn't matter, Mom. Grayson just wanted me to go on the road with him."

Peggy's eyes widened. "He proposed?"

Was her mother listening at all? "Propositioned, more like." She didn't want to think how close she'd been to joining him in Red Rock. Because from there, how easy would it have been to agree to all the rest? "But don't worry." Her throat felt tight. "I know better than to become a Grayson Groupie."

Peggy didn't look convinced. "I think you're still crazy for him. Same way you were when you were Selena's age."

She'd been sixteen, not thirteen, but she knew there was little point in correcting that particular detail.

"Grayson was only a client." Maybe if she said the words often enough, she would start to believe it. "And now he's not. There's nothing more to say about it." She reached for the door once more, only to have it fly open before she could touch it.

Selena grabbed her arm. "Come on. You gotta see."

"The only thing I've gotta do is get something to drink," she countered.

But her young cousin held on. "No, you gotta come." She was aiming toward the inflatable pool where Ray's oldest, Meredith, was floating on her back in the two feet of water.

"Hi, Aunt Billie." Meredith kicked her legs, splashing water over the side of the pool as well as Billie's T-shirt. "Oh, sorry."

Billie managed a smile. There would come a day when she wasn't reminded of Grayson everywhere she turned, but it certainly wasn't going to be that day.

Selena kept pulling her past the pool to the folding chairs surrounding the television propped on its usual sawed-off tree stump. It was the same stump that had supported a TV even when Billie was Selena's age.

"Watch." Selena pushed her toward one of the empty chairs. "They'll show it again, for sure."

Billie resisted. She really, really didn't want to see any of the rodeo. And that could be the only reason her cousin was so insistent. "When did you get taller than me? I'm sure you weren't as tall as me at your birthday party."

"Peanut." Ray had joined the others around the television and he put his hand on her shoulder. "Maybe you should watch."

Billie's mouth felt dry. But the only thing she saw when Selena crouched down on the grass near the television and turned up the volume was a beer commercial. At least it wasn't one of Grayson's. "Thrilling." She tried to turn away.

"Wait."

She exhaled impatiently. "Look, guys. I don't want to see Grayson beat Max. Or Max beat Grayson. Or anyone else beat both of them. I do *not*—" She broke off when the commercial ended and a shot of a rodeo arena filled the screen.

Her stomach tightened.

But it quickly became obvious that it was the tie-down event that was under way. Not steer wrestling at all.

The knots in her stomach began to ease up. "Travis Conrad," she said, as she recognized the competitor. "Max's buddy. Oops." On the screen, the calf had escaped his ties.

"No time for Travis. Bummer." The double zeros flashed on the screen while the rodeo announcer stirred up the crowd to applaud anyway as Travis rode out of the arena.

Before Billie had a chance to look away again, the image flashed to a picture of an ambulance pulling out of the dirt arena. "That there's the fine folks who're gonna transport another one of our Texas boys to the hospital," the announcer drawled. As she watched, the image of the ambulance was replaced by another video clip.

And then she *couldn't* look away.

Just stood there in horror, watching.

Grayson. Flying through the air as he slid from his horse toward the running steer. Only the steer stopped short, and instead of finding purchase on the animal, Grayson slid right past him, landing in a tangle of racing horse legs and steer horns. The hazer's horse went down, rolling right over him, and both animals became even more frenzied as they tried to get away from each other, from Grayson and from the riders who raced in trying to separate them all.

And once they succeeded, instead of rolling to his feet the way she'd watched in countless videos, Grayson just lay there on the ground.

"There's a steer-wrestling wreck if there ever was

one," the announcer said as the very worst of the video started playing again. As if once wasn't enough. "Now, folks, we all know accidents can happen despite everything we do to keep our rodeo athletes safe, but you combine a five-hundred-pound steer and horses going thirty miles an hour and—"

Billie's head seemed to fill with a roaring sound as the video went to slow motion on his cowboy hat rolling from Grayson and finally falling flat amid a cloud of dust.

"—all remember six years ago, Grayson used to compete in saddle bronc, until injuries during the National Finals in Las Vegas sidelined—"

She bolted away from the rodeo announcer's voice and ran into the house, where she'd left her purse.

"Belinda—"

She ignored her mother's call. Once inside, she fumbled in her purse for her cell phone, only to finally upend the contents right on the kitchen counter. Her keys, notes about property listings, lipstick and commission check all scattered. She snatched her phone from the midst of it and quickly found Deborah Fortune's number and dialed.

She wasn't even aware of her mother hovering beside her as the phone rang, until Peggy pushed a chair against the back of her knees and made her sit on it.

Finally, the call was answered. "He's okay, Billie," Deborah said in greeting, sounding breathless.

Billie's insides liquefied. She leaned over, until her head was near her knees. "You're not just saying that? I saw the replay on television."

"The doctor at the arena is pretty certain he's broken a bone or two. But he was conscious and, of course, mad as hell at himself. There's a pilot here who is giving us a lift to the hospital in Lubbock."

She was still ready to think the worst. "He *was* conscious?"

"They've given him something for the pain," Deborah said. She sounded far calmer than Billie felt. "He was asking for you."

Billie lifted her head again. "What?"

"Honey, I know it's a lot to ask, but would you consider meeting us at the hospital?"

Her knots tightened up again. "Why would he a-ask for me? The ranch sale is complete."

"There was a time when I was as single-minded as you." Deborah sounded disappointed. "I guess I wanted to believe there was more between the two of you than—"

"I can get to Lubbock." The decision came out in a rush, so easily it was really no decision at all. "I'll fly or drive. If...if you're really sure he wants me there."

"I'm very sure." Deborah didn't wait a beat. "We'll be in Lubbock within the hour. If you do drive, be careful yourself. The last thing we want is another accident."

"I'll be careful. Mrs. Fortune—Deborah—thank you." Billie's hands were shaking as she ended the call and opened the flight app on her phone. The next flight to Lubbock didn't leave for a few hours, and it was routed through Houston before backtracking to Lubbock. Meaning it was unlikely she'd save any time at all traveling by air.

She pushed to her feet and slid her phone into her pocket. "I'm driving."

"I'll go with you," Peggy said quietly.

Tears burned in her eyes. "Mom."

"You're not driving all that way when you're this upset." She began shoveling the contents of Billie's purse back inside. When she reached the commission check, she hesitated, her eyes widening when she saw the amount. She carefully tucked the check inside the purse and then cupped Billie's chin in her hand. "I warned you that life doesn't follow all the little plans we make."

"The day isn't complete without an 'I told you so' from Mom," Ray said as he walked into the kitchen.

"Because so many days go by when I'm right about so much," Peggy retorted. "Now, I'll just go tell Hal and we'll get on our way."

"It's okay." Billie swiped at her face. "You don't have to ride with me, Mom. We'd just have to figure out how to get you back home again. You know you hate to fly." She gave Peggy a tight hug. "But thank you for offering." She kissed cheek. "I'll call you when I get to Lubbock."

Peggy looked like she wanted to argue. But then, surprisingly, she subsided. "All right."

Billie couldn't contain her surprise. "That's all you're going to say?"

"Well." Her mother handed her the refilled purse. "When all this is over, I guess maybe we'll let you buy us a new air-conditioning unit, after all."

It was nearly dark by the time Billie reached the emergency center parking lot in Lubbock. She'd made the drive in just under six hours. But before leaving town, she'd gone to her apartment to throw some clothes in an overnight bag. She'd phoned Amberleigh from the road to have her reschedule her appointments for the rest of the week, and only thoughts of Grayson's comments on her lead foot kept her from hitting the gas pedal even harder.

She'd kept the radio on the news stations the whole while, but didn't hear anything at all about him. Not that it surprised her. A rodeo accident generally didn't garner the same media attention that other sporting event catastrophes did. Which meant that for a good portion of her drive, she was entirely out of touch with both ends, Lubbock and Austin.

She locked the car and hurried through the emergency room doors. She figured that she'd have to ask someone to find Grayson's mother first, but the moment she walked through the waiting area to the information desk, she stopped in her tracks, hopeful emotion flooding her at the sight of him standing right there. "Grayson?"

As soon as she said his name, the tall man turned to look.

Disappointment flooded through her. How stupid of her.

It wasn't Grayson at all. Just a near identical version of him. His brother. Either Jayden or Nathan.

The man headed toward her, one hand outstretched. "You're Billie."

She nodded. She felt more than a little punch-drunk with the combination of worry, the long drive and now, feeling like she was seeing double. "You're—"

"Jayden." The man smiled faintly as he squeezed her hand. He hitched his thumb toward the carbon copy who'd walked up beside him. "And this is Nate."

She looked from one face to the next. They were equally as handsome as Grayson. But she didn't feel a speck of the pull that their brother held for her. "How's Grayson?"

"Loopy as all hell," Nathan answered. "He just got out of surgery and the anesthetic's still wearing off. Keeps talking about getting some damn shoes or something."

"Probably got the deal he just inked with Castleton Boots still on his brain," Jayden surmised. "Anyway..." He turned his attention to Billie again. "Mom sent us down here to wait for you. There's not a lot of space in the recovery room." As if he recognized the fact that her knees had turned rubbery, Jayden slid a supportive arm around her shoulders. "They had to put a pin or two in his leg and he's got a concussion. Docs say he might not remember everything that's happened, but he'll heal up okay."

"Except he's not gonna be bulldogging for a while," Nathan added. His voice was a little deeper than Jayden's. His expression a little more closed. "Not the rest of this season, anyway."

She realized that as the men had talked, Jayden had steered her to the elevators.

"He's not going to be happy about that," she said faintly. "I don't think he's ready to retire, even though he's been thinking about it."

"Retire!" Both brothers looked shocked, and she caught the glance passing between them as she stepped into the waiting elevator.

"He's talked to you about that?" Jayden punched the button for the third floor as the doors slid shut.

"I didn't know it was secret."

"It's not," Jayden assured her. "Just didn't know he'd talked to anyone about it besides me and Nate and Mom."

Billie chewed the inside of her lip. She wasn't sure if Grayson's brother was happy about that fact or not. And it made for a very slow climb from the first to the third floor as silence bounced around the elevator car.

Finally, the doors opened again, and the two men waited for her to exit first. Then took a circuitous route until they stopped outside one of several curtained cubicles fanning out from a central nurses' station.

Billie's nerves were at fever pitch. She started to reach for the curtain, but her hand froze in midair. People said all sorts of things when they were under the influence of painkillers and anesthetics.

"You all right, kiddo?"

She looked up at Jayden. "When my dad had shoulder surgery a few years ago, he thought he was an astronaut on a space mission."

His expression softened, making him look even more like Grayson. "You've come this far."

"Might as well go the distance," Nathan added.

She swallowed. "I hate feeling like a ninny," she muttered.

"You're not a ninny. It just ain't all that easy falling in love with a Fortune."

Startled, she stared at Jayden. Nobody had said anything about *love*. "I've only known your brother for a few weeks."

He definitely wasn't cowed by her stare. If anything, he looked like he wanted to smile. "Sometimes that's all it takes."

Nathan nodded toward the curtain. "We're not here to make you go in, Billie. If you've changed your mind, change it now rather than later."

He couldn't have chosen better words to straighten her shoulders. She pulled back the edge of the curtain far enough to see the foot of the hospital bed. A lot of thick white cast extending up and over his knee. A lot of bare, masculine thigh. And a very little bit of white sheet between thigh and hair-dusted chest.

She felt perspiration break out along her spine.

Then Deborah stepped forward, rounding the end of the bed and catching Billie's hands in her own. "Billie, hon." She brushed her cheek against Billie's. "I'm so glad to see you." She gently tugged her into the curtained room.

Billie decided then and there that Grayson's brothers looked more like him than he did lying there right now. His eyes were closed. His face was so pale that the bruises on his temple and his cheek looked purple in contrast.

Deborah drew her unresistingly to the side of the bed. "Grayson, honey, look who's here."

Billie swallowed her instinctive protest not to wake him, and felt afraid to breathe as she waited for Grayson's eyes to open. Waited for him to look at her with the same anger that he'd felt for her in Reno.

"Mom." Jayden quietly caught Deborah's attention. He and Nathan were still standing just outside the border of the cubicle. They'd been joined by an older man with salt-and-pepper hair who struck Billie as vaguely familiar. "Orlando is flying back to Horseback Hollow. Now that everything's stable here, we figured we'd hitch a ride with him and leave the truck here for you."

"Excuse me, hon." Deborah left Billie's side and joined them. "I know you want to get back to Ariana and Bianca." The curtain rattled softly in its track as she pulled it closed behind her .

Billie tuned out their low voices, which were still audible despite the impression of privacy afforded by the curtain, and sank down on the chair next to the bed. She moistened her dry lips, looking from Grayson's ashen face to the monitors surrounding him. One beeping softly. One humming monotonously. He had an IV taped to one arm and some sort of sensor clipped over the tip of his index finger. The leg with the cast from the knee down was suspended several inches off the mattress by an overhead contraption.

"Grayson," she whispered tentatively.

He didn't stir.

Her eyes burned and it felt like a vise had tightened around her throat. "I'm so sorry I didn't tell you about Max. That I didn't believe he was wrong about Bethany without you having to say it. I'm sorry I didn't tell you that I would have gone to Red Rock with you." Unable to help herself, she leaned even closer to the bed. "Or anywhere else," she added hoarsely. "Just open your eyes so I know you're really okay." She slid her hand beneath his on the mattress and her heartbeat stuttered when his lax fingers seemed to tighten against hers. "Grayson? Wake up, sweetheart, please."

"Anywhere." His lips barely moved.

She could hardly breathe. "What?"

"You'll go anywhere." The words weren't much more than a mumble. His thick eyelashes lifted only long enough for her to glimpse a thin slice of dark brown.

But it was enough.

Tears burned in her eyes and she pressed her forehead to his hand, aching sobs jerking through her body.

His hand moved. Pulled away from hers. But only to touch her hair. And then he was still again. When she looked at him, his eyes were closed once more.

But the monitors were beeping softly. Humming reassuringly.

She wiped her face, but the tears still flowed. Not because she'd been saving them up for so many years.

But because he was the kind of man who really could—and would—break her heart.

Chapter Twelve

"Say hello to Selena." Billie turned her phone to face Grayson so that her cousin could see his face.

Grayson offered his trademark grin. "Hello, Selena. How's the riding clinic going?"

On the small screen, Selena's face was beaming. "Great! I'm trying to talk my mom and dad into buying a horse, but they keep saying no way."

Billie tapped her fingers against the edge of Grayson's cast, which was propped on the chair next to her. They were sitting at the kitchen table at his family ranch in Paseo, as they had each morning since he'd been released from the hospital. "I warned you that she'd end up wanting her own horse," she stated. He'd helped her young cousin get enrolled in one of Grayson Good's ongoing riding clinics in Austin.

"I do, but it's okay," Selena said. "Long as I get to ride Molly at the clinic, I'm still happy. She's the best horse

ever! My mom and dad said I had to write you a thank-
you letter." She held up a small rectangle that had a big
pink heart drawn on it. "But I already did. We're gonna
mail it today."

"I'm glad you're having fun, darlin'."

The sun could have taken lessons from the wattage in
Selena's smile. "Are you gonna be back in Austin soon?"

Billie chewed the inside of her cheek, waiting for
Grayson to answer. Even though Mr. Allen was salivat-
ing over Austin Elite handling the commercial property
search for Grayson Gear, she figured her boss's good
graces would only go so far. She'd already been away
from the real estate office for nearly a month now while
Grayson recuperated. His purchase of the Harmon ranch
was complete, but the house was still empty, and he'd
chosen to come back to Paseo. It was just easier, he'd said.

Privately, Billie had wondered if he was testing her
to see if she really would go with him.

If so, she'd wanted to pass that test. So when he'd been
released from the hospital, she'd offered to drive him the
long way to his hometown of Paseo. He'd be more comfortable in the big back seat of her car than in the pickup
or the private charter plane that Orlando Mendoza—
who'd been the one to fly him from Cowboy Country to
Lubbock—had offered.

It was only later that Billie had realized why he'd
looked familiar.

Because he'd been the man with Lady Whatsername
at La Viña the night she'd had dinner there with Grayson. Lady Whatsername who was really Lady Josephine
Fortune Chesterfield and a relative of Grayson's, albeit
a distant one.

That hadn't stopped Lady Fortune Chesterfield and
her fiancé, Orlando, from inviting Grayson and his fam-

ily to their wedding, being held in a few weeks. The invitation was taped to the old-fashioned white refrigerator because Deborah had already accepted. They owed Orlando a debt of gratitude, she'd said, considering the way he'd helped after Grayson's accident.

It was one small mystery solved. But after three weeks of being in Paseo, a larger one loomed. Because she didn't really know why Grayson wanted her there.

And she couldn't help but feel increasingly antsy.

Deborah told her to have patience. That Grayson had never trusted easily, and the fact that he'd wanted Billie with him in Paseo meant more than any words he wasn't offering.

She hadn't known what to expect when they'd arrived at the remote ranch. She knew that Jayden and his wife lived there. As did Nathan and Bianca and little EJ. And Deborah. If Billie had thought all the bodies there would mean little extra space for her, she'd been wrong.

Grayson hadn't even suggested that she sleep with him. Instead, she was in a small room of her own that had a chair and a window. She'd spent a lot of long nights sleeping alone in a narrow bed, knowing he was only a few doors away.

She looked at him now as he spoke with her niece. "We'll be in Austin next week," he answered Selena. "Have an appointment with the orthopedist."

"Are you gonna get outta your cast?"

He made a face. "Probably not just yet. But maybe they'll give me a smaller one." His gaze slid over Billie. "Something easier to maneuver around with."

All sorts of warmth sprang out inside her, but she knew better than to get too excited, considering he'd been treating her pretty much the same way he treated his sisters-in-law, Ariana and Bianca. Like a sister.

It was maddening.

Frustrating.

And confusing as anything in her life had ever been.

"That'd be cool," Selena was saying. "When will you be able to start riding again?"

Billie tucked her tongue between her teeth. She was more anxious to hear the answer than Selena could possibly be.

"I'd ride right now if I could get myself on the back of a horse, but the crutches tend to get in the way."

Selena giggled. "I mean *rodeo* riding."

Grayson's grin stayed in place, though Billie thought it looked forced. "Don't really know, Selena. That's up to the doctors, still."

The girl made a face. "Well, I hope it's soon. You know Max's head is getting, like, *this* big." She held her hands in the air, so wide apart the phone screen couldn't capture them. "He's winnin' every week, seems like."

"Good for him," Grayson said smoothly.

"He'll never be as great as you, though," Selena assured him, ever loyal despite being related to Max.

"Never say never," Grayson warned. "Your cousin's just startin' out. And I'm…" He shrugged. "Well, I'm laid up with a dang cast on my leg that's itching me like crazy."

Selena wrinkled her nose. "My dad had a cast on his arm last year. It got stinky, too, 'cause he kept getting it wet. Billie, you're not letting Grayson's cast get wet, are you?"

"Grayson's a big boy." Billie ignored the flush in her face. "It's up to him to keep his cast from getting wet."

"But I thought you were there helpin' him."

"She is," Grayson answered easily, into Billie's stymied silence. "In fact, she's gonna help me out to the barn now because whether I can ride 'em or not, I've still got to take care of Vix and Van. So say goodbye to Selena, Billie."

"Goodbye, Selena," she said obediently.

Her cousin waved at them, smiling broadly. "Bye, Billie. Bye, Grayson." A moment later, the screen went black.

Billie set aside the cell phone. "Thanks for not bad-mouthing Max to Selena." He still wasn't talking to her, no doubt even more entrenched in his opinion since she'd run to Grayson's hospital bedside.

Grayson's lips tightened. "Do you think I'd really do that?"

She handed him his crutches. "I don't know what I think." She moved over to the kitchen door and looked out. She could see the barn that Ariana had told her had been damaged the year before during the tornado but now looked in perfect condition. It was going to be hot that afternoon, so the doors were closed to keep in the air-conditioning. But she could still hear the tinkle of the wind chimes hanging near the door that Jayden kept outside to help orient his blind dog, Sugar.

As she watched, she saw the dog and EJ both running across the patch of grass growing on one side of the barn.

Grayson's new nephew was four. He was a brown-haired ball of energy and Billie wasn't the least bit surprised when she saw Bianca running after her son a few moments later. Then Nate caught them all, and soon they were tumbling on the ground, rolling in the grass.

The three of them so clearly belonged together, the sight made Billie ache inside. Even though both Ariana and Bianca had been incredibly welcoming to her, Billie still knew that *they* belonged here in Paseo, in this incredibly charming but modest ranch house, with their husbands.

Billie was just…she didn't know what.

She looked back at the man responsible for all the uncertainty stirring inside her. If he'd made even a single attempt to kiss her, or to touch her, just once in the last twenty-one days, she wouldn't have felt so adrift. But he hadn't. And it wasn't because he was too unfit with his broken leg.

For heaven's sake, just yesterday afternoon she'd watched him working alongside his two brothers, tossing bales of hay that outweighed her, keeping pace with both of them. All three men had been shirtless and sweating. The only difference was that Jayden and Nathan each had two good jean-clad legs. Grayson had a casted leg sticking out of the jeans he'd torn up one side to accommodate the bulk, while the crutches he was supposed to be using had been tossed aside.

Ariana, who'd been washing dishes at the sink while Billie dried, had nearly been drooling as she'd watched her husband out the window. "Hard to believe there are three of them, isn't it?"

Billie hadn't even been able to articulate agreement.

"Three, four, five, six," EJ had chirped from the table, where he and his mom were looking at a picture book.

Ariana and Bianca had laughed. Billie had had to excuse herself to go off and take a walk. It was either that or a cold shower. And she'd figured a walk would draw less interest, considering how many people shared the limited number of bathrooms in the house.

She could still hear EJ's peals of laughter from outside now as she watched Grayson stand up from the table, fitting the crutches under his arms before heading toward her. Toward the door.

But when she didn't move out of the way, he raised an eyebrow. "What?"

Her heart suddenly felt like it was beating inside her throat. She reached up and slid her hand behind his neck, pulling his head down to hers, boldly fastening her lips to his.

She felt his surprise.

Then his resistance.

Determined not to quail, she added another arm around him, fitting herself tightly against him.

Then he swore, angled his head a little and kissed her back.

One of his crutches clattered noisily against the kitchen counter and bounced off onto the ground as his hand slid behind her back. It traveled beneath the edge of her T-shirt and splayed hotly against her skin.

He tasted like the coffee Ariana had made that morning. Like the peach-studded pancakes that Bianca had prepared. Like maple syrup and the kind of hope that made Billie long to roll around laughing in the grass with him and a boy of their own.

His other crutch clattered against the tile and his hands grasped her arms.

At first, she thought it was just to keep his balance. But she realized quickly enough that he was pulling her hands away. That he was dragging his mouth from hers. Putting distance between them.

His overlong hair was messed, his dark eyes burning between his thick lashes. But it was her breath that was coming fast, as if she'd been running sprints.

Which pretty much described how she'd felt since meeting him. One breathless sprint after another.

"What am I doing here, Grayson?"

His brows pulled together. Instead of answering, he

leaned down, balancing on one leg, and scooped up a crutch, which he stuffed under his arm. Then he reached around her to pull open the door. She knew he wasn't unaffected by their kiss because she could see the evidence for herself. "Horses need exercising." His voice sounded gruff.

She opened her mouth to protest, but didn't know what to say.

Instead, she just watched him clomp out the door, then down the porch steps and toward the barn, seeming to barely even nod an acknowledgment when he crossed paths with Bianca, who was heading for the house.

Billie nudged the door closed and turned away, trying to gather her composure before Bianca could see her.

She might as well have tried jumping over the moon.

As soon as Grayson's newest sister-in-law floated into the kitchen and saw Billie, her eyebrows pulled together. "Honey! What's wrong?"

Billie sank down onto a chair, covering her face. "Nothing." Ever since she'd cried at Grayson's bedside, her tears came much too easily. "Everything."

Bianca snatched a napkin from the holder on the table and pressed it into her hand. "You want to talk about it?"

Billie knew that Bianca was only a few years older than she was. That she already had one failed marriage under her belt, and that she was the little sister of Nathan's best friend, who'd died while he and Nate had been in the military together.

"Not really." Billie swiped at her cheeks, her nose. Then she crumpled the napkin in her fist and proceeded to talk, anyway. "I don't understand him." She grabbed another napkin. "At all. People say women are complicated. But our sex has *nothing* on men."

Bianca smiled sympathetically. "Particularly Fortune men."

"At least Nathan made it plain what he wanted from you! You're married. You and EJ are making a family with him."

"True, but it wasn't as if he just arrived at that conclusion all that easily." Bianca tucked her long hair behind her ear. "At first I didn't think he wanted me, even though he took EJ and me in when we had nowhere else to turn. We lived here in this house with him, but he never took advantage of it. He was very…old-fashioned about it at first."

Billie studied the other woman. "Old-fashioned. As in…"

"He didn't touch me for what seemed the longest time," Bianca said. "Didn't matter how much chemistry we had. Not that I was anxious to move too fast, either, but—" She broke off, smiling ruefully.

"Is it a family trait, then?" Billie scrubbed her cheeks. "Or is it just that Grayson likes the chase better than the actual catch?"

"I can't speak for Grayson, obviously. I'd barely even met him before he was injured. Nathan and I had some stuff to work through. With my brother's death. Then my ex-husband. Ariana and Jayden, too, had to find a way through the fact that she was planning to write about them being the latest secret sons of Gerald Robinson. But the point is, we all found our way."

"How?" Billie pushed to her feet and paced the length of the kitchen and back. "I don't know how to reach him if he won't talk. Or touch."

"The only thing I know is you can't give up when something really matters." Bianca pulled a few juice boxes from the refrigerator. "Does Grayson really matter?"

Billie exhaled. "More than I want him to."

"There's your answer." Bianca held up the juices. "Nathan and EJ want to go for a walk. You're welcome to join us."

Billie managed a smile. "Thanks, but you guys go." She knew it wasn't all that often that Nathan or Jayden had any downtime around the ranch. "Enjoy."

Bianca gave her an encouraging smile. "Keep your chin up, Billie. When things are meant to work out, they seem to do just that."

And when they weren't meant to?

She kept the thought to herself as the other woman left, then nearly jumped out of her skin when the wall phone rang shrilly.

There was no one in the house besides her. Deborah had gone into town before breakfast. Ariana and Jayden had gone off after breakfast to visit some people who lived nearby. "Nearby," Billie had learned, was a relative term, since nothing was really nearby in this remote area of the world. The only reason Billie's cell phone had worked since coming to Paseo was because the town had recently bowed to pressure from some of its residents to put up a cell tower. Until then, the area had been a landline-only sort of place.

The phone kept ringing and she finally reached out, plucking the old-fashioned receiver off the hook. "Fortune residence."

"May I speak with Grayson, please?" The voice was feminine. Throaty. "This is Bethany Belmont."

Billie's fingers tightened on the hard plastic receiver. "He's not in the house right at the moment. Do you want to hold on while I get him?"

"No, that's okay. Is this Deborah?"

"No. She's out, too."

"Oh, well. Would you be able to take down a message for me?"

Billie's jaw felt so stiff it was hard to speak. "Sure."

"Tell him it's going to be a boy. And I, uh, I've thought about what he told me and decided he's right. He'll know what I mean. Have you got that?"

Just what she wanted to do. Deliver messages with inside meanings. "I've got it."

"Thanks. And tell him thanks, too, will you please?"

Billie twisted the coiled cord in her fist. It was wrong to imagine it was Bethany's hair she was pulling, but she did so, anyway. And she wondered what Bethany would say if Billie told her she was Max Vargas's cousin.

"I'll tell him. G'bye." She quickly hung up before her baser instincts took control. Grayson was right—whatever had gone on between Max and the pregnant barrel racer was their business.

Billie exhaled and went outside to deal with her and Grayson's business.

When she reached the barn, it was pretty obvious that he'd had no intention of waiting for her or anyone else to help him with the horses. Because there he was, leaning on one crutch while still managing to wield a pitchfork to spread straw across a stall. Nearby was a wheelbarrow full of the manure and straw he'd obviously already mucked out.

She went over and took the pitchfork from his hand. "You're getting your cast filthy. What if you get an infection or something?"

"We'll never know, 'cause I'm gonna saw the damn thing off if it doesn't stop itching me."

"Maybe your skin wouldn't itch so much if you didn't insist on being Mr. Ranch Man right alongside your able-bodied brothers! You're a terrible patient, you know. Your mom warned me before we left the hospital, and she was right."

Billie finished spreading the straw and turned to the next stall. She grabbed the shovel and scraped it along the floor, dragging out the mess that needed to be cleared first. "Bethany called to tell you that it's a boy." *Scrape, scrape.* "That she thought about what you said and you're right." *Muck, muck.* "You'd know what that meant. And thanks." She pitched the crap into the wheelbarrow and went back for another shovelful.

He was looking at her warily. "That's it?"

She dumped the second shovelful, as well. "Are you expecting another meltdown from me?"

"I'm not sure what to expect from you."

She smiled humorlessly. "That makes two of us, then." She went back for a third shovel, scraping the ground meticulously clean before considering it ready for fresh straw. Doing exactly what she'd learned all those years ago when she'd worked at Rodeo Austin, hoping for a glimpse of the Big G. The Great Grayson.

"You know," she said, as she dumped the last shovelful and grabbed the pitchfork, "I still have a calendar that you signed for me when I was sixteen. I remember everything about that day as clearly as if it were yesterday."

"I'm glad I don't remember."

She winced. "Well. Thanks for that."

"It would just remind me how young you are."

She propped her arm on top of the pitchfork handle and eyed him. "I'm no younger now than I was a month ago when you were trying seduction by shoe. Pretty effectively, too, except that I didn't want to get my butt fired from my new job. The job I've now basically put on hold for you, anyway. Do you want me here or don't you, Grayson? Because I honestly don't know!"

He grabbed the pitchfork, looking impatient. "If I hadn't wanted you here, I would've said so."

"But I have no purpose here!" She waved her hand at him. "You're clearly not in need of a nursemaid. Even if you were, you'd blow it off because you're *The* Grayson. Gotta prove you're all manly-man, even when you've still got bruises from being trampled by two horses and a steer. And you're clearly not in need of a bedmate, or you wouldn't have put me in a separate bedroom!"

"For Christ's sake, Billie. My mother lives in this house, too. What do you want us to do? Get down and dirty right on the kitchen table? I've never let another woman come here with me. Not like this." He raked his fingers through his hair. "You know I want you. But I also don't want to make a mistake that'll end up hurting you!"

She stared at him. "You think I'm not afraid of making a mistake?"

"You've got a normal family, Billie. You don't have to worry that you'll turn out like your bastard of a father!"

"Grayson!"

At the sound of a new voice, they both whirled, to find Deborah standing in the doorway of the barn. She looked pale. But no more so than the tall, commanding-looking man with a head of thick gray hair and Grayson's brown eyes standing there with her.

Billie's stomach fell to her toes as she looked from Gerald Robinson's face to Grayson's.

"What the hell are *you* doing here?" he demanded.

Gerald looked at Deborah.

She lifted her chin slightly. "I invited him," she said clearly.

Grayson's knuckles were white where he was clenching the pitchfork. So white that Billie took a concerned step toward him. Whether because she was afraid he'd pitch the thing across the barn at his father, or because he was still recovering from surgery he'd had less than a month ago, she didn't know.

But it didn't matter.

Because the second she took that step, his head swiveled toward her. *"Don't,"* he gritted.

She froze. "Don't what? Don't touch you? Don't worry for you? Don't love you?" Her eyes flooded with tears and she spread her hands. "Too late for that mistake. Too bad that you asked for me in the hospital. All of this could have been avoided." She'd still be wishing for things that would never be, but at least she'd have never fallen in love with Paseo and the rest of his family, too.

"You're the one who came to the hospital," he said through his teeth. "I woke up and there you were. Strange, but I thought that meant something."

She heard a rushing sound in her head. The only other time she'd experienced it was when she'd been watching the replay of his rodeo accident on television. "You didn't ask for me…" A part of her was aware of Deborah walking toward them.

"Grayson, honey, you had a concussion. They said you might not remember everything that happened that day. But you most certainly did ask for Billie."

He glared at Robinson, who'd followed Deborah. "I remember *he* was in the grandstands. Just like you were in Reno," he said to the man. "Weren't you?"

Gerald inclined his head slightly. "I was there."

Grayson rounded on his mother. "You told me you hadn't seen him in Reno."

"She hadn't." Gerald put his hand on Deborah's shoulder, which seemed to infuriate Grayson even more.

Despite everything, Billie edged closer to him, touching his arm. "Grayson, why don't you sit down?"

"Dammit, Billie!" He shrugged her off. "This doesn't concern you!"

If he'd physically slapped her, it would have hurt less.

She swallowed hard. "You're right." She'd known he would be the kind of man who could break her heart. And even knowing it, she'd still let it happen.

She gave Deborah a painful smile and stepped around her and Gerald.

The only thing she could concentrate on was escape. So that's what she did.

"You're making a huge mistake, son."

Grayson's molars ground together. He looked from where Billie no longer was to his mother. "The mistake was thinking that *you* would never lie to us. But you did. First about us not having a father. Second about our last name. Third—" he gestured at Robinson, whose presence there was enough to make him want to choke "—about getting involved with him again!"

"We're not involved." His mother's voice was tight.

"Really?" Grayson looked at Gerald's face. "He know that?"

"I know you're angry, Grayson," he said.

At least the old man hadn't called him *son*. "You think?" He threw the pitchfork aside and the sharp prongs dug into a wood post.

"I never knew that your mother was pregnant with you. If I had—"

Grayson cut him off. "And you never knew about all the other women you left pregnant, either, I bet." He advanced on Gerald, moving unevenly because of the damned cast. "The women who started coming outta the woodwork as soon as your favored son, Ben, started looking for all of us poor slobs who got left out in the cold once everyone learned you weren't who you said you were. *Jerome*."

"Grayson—"

"Just because I never talk about it doesn't mean I didn't listen. You didn't want to marry any of 'em except one. The fair Charlotte Prendergast Robinson who—after you'd already abandoned *my* mom—gave you eight legitimate little Robinsons. Or are they really Fortunes, since that's who you really are? It's a little hard to keep straight." Grayson stopped when he got six inches from Gerald's nose. Looked him straight in the eye. "Not my mom. Not Nash's mom. Or Amersen's. Or Chloe's. How many others are there, *Dad*?"

Deborah pushed between them. "Stop this right now! You don't know the whole story, Grayson."

"I don't need to know." He looked at his mom. She'd been the linchpin of their family. Made of leather and steel. Jayden said she'd always had to be, raising three sons on her own in Texas the way she had. "You didn't know he was in Reno. Fine. Did you know he was at Cowboy Country?"

He didn't need to hear the answer when he could see it in her eyes.

"Yeah." He shook his head. "That's what I thought."

Then he, too, limped out of the barn.

He intended to head to the house.

Mend fences with Billie. If he could.

But the second he left the barn, he knew he'd lost that chance, too.

Because her big, old-lady luxury car was gone. And knowing the way she drove, she'd be outta the county in minutes.

His leg ached and his balance wobbled. He threw out his arm, intending to grab the side of the barn.

He got human instead of wood and he swore all over again.

As soon as he'd steadied him, Gerald stepped away. "I didn't intend for you to see me in Reno *or* Cowboy Country."

"Too freaking late."

The older man's lips tightened. "I hope that wasn't a factor in your accident."

"The only factor in my accident was thinking about a woman when I should've been thinking about the steer."

"The woman who just left?"

"I'm not talking about Billie with you. I'm not talking about anything with you."

Gerald nodded. "Fair enough. I'll just tell you one thing. I heard what you said. That you don't want to be like your bastard father. Then don't be like me. If you really love this girl, go after her. Or spend the rest of your life like I have, chasing a taste of happiness that, unfortunately, you'll never find again."

"If that's supposed to mean you loved my mother, sell it to the next guy. I'm not buying."

"You don't have to buy it, Grayson." Gerald looked to where Deborah had come out of the barn, as well. Her arms were folded across her chest and her expression said she wasn't particularly pleased with either one of them. "But it doesn't make it any less true."

Chapter Thirteen

He saw Billie the second he walked into Twine.

Hard not to, when she was in the middle of the dance floor, a blur of short white dress and flying dark hair as she jumped up and down to some song that he'd never heard before. Aside from the visceral appeal of watching her move the way she was, he pretty much hoped he'd never hear the song again. 'Cause it would just remind him of the leer on the face of the guy who *was* dancing with her.

It had been only five days since she'd driven away from him and Paseo. Five days for him to sulk, as his mom had plainly put it. More like five days for him to get over the burning anger he felt every time he thought about his mother actually inviting the man who'd betrayed her to their house.

At which point, Deborah promptly pointed out that the Paseo ranch was still her home and she had every right to invite whomever she wanted. Particularly when

Grayson had a new home that he needed to be concerned with. Including the fact that, if he didn't get over his almighty sulk where Billie's leaving was concerned, he'd be living in it all alone.

He waded into the fray of writhing dancers, cursing under his breath when someone gasped and grabbed his arm. "Ohmygod. You're Grayson!" The someone was red-haired and dancing so frenetically her dress was practically falling off her shoulders. She shimmied even closer to him and he hastily sidled away, not moving as quickly as he wanted because of the stiff boot wrapped around his new half cast. He bumped into a tall guy who didn't even seem to notice, then finally managed to make his way to Billie.

She stopped dead in her tracks when he stepped between her and her dance partner.

One glance and it was obvious that she'd been drinking. Not that it took much. He'd learned that the night they'd been at La Viña. Two glasses of wine was all it had taken and she'd been toast.

"What're you doing here?"

"What do you think?"

She turned up her nose and her back, and started dancing again. This time with the two women behind her.

Once again, he stepped in her way.

She glared and shoved her hair out of her face. It was loose and straight and slid silkily down her back, just waiting for his hands to tangle in it. "How'd you know I was here?"

"Max."

That, at least, gave her pause. For about ten seconds. Then she turned her back once more and started dancing yet again.

He sighed, wondering how long it would be before

the song ended. Only to realize quickly enough that the song wasn't going to end for the simple reason that the DJ spun straight into another hard-beating tune.

Grayson had spent the morning with the orthopedist talking his way around to the walking boot. Then signing autographs at a Grayson Gear-Castleton Boots event where his manager, Jess, had decided it was a brilliant idea to have the newest up-and-comer, Max Vargas, also sign autographs. As a marketing ploy, Grayson could understand it.

Out with the old. In with the new.

But what he hadn't been able to understand was Max willingly participating.

That is, until he'd seen Bethany, looking way more pregnant than she had the last time he'd seen her, standing in the wings. Then he'd remembered the message that Billie had relayed that last day in Paseo. That Bethany had decided he'd been right.

The only thing he'd told her was that it wasn't fair for a kid to never know his dad.

Which meant Max, ready or not, was going to be a father.

When Max had sat down at the table beside him, his apology had been begrudging. But Grayson had to at least give the kid credit for offering it.

He wasn't sure he'd have done the same in his position.

When Grayson had finally peeled away from the event, he'd wished them both good luck. Bethany had kissed his cheek, still grateful for the job at the Grayson Gear office. Max had told him that Billie had taken to going out to Twine every night. Then he'd shoved his hands in his back pockets and told him that if Grayson hurt his cousin more than he already had, all bets were off.

Billie was gyrating in front of him, her short dress

barely skimming the backs of her smooth thighs. And he'd had enough.

He wrapped his arm around her and flipped her up and over his shoulder.

"What the *hell*!" She thumped his back. Hard. "Put me down."

He clamped his arm over her thighs, holding her sorry excuse of a dress down over her butt, and started working his way off the dance floor. One young woman looked startled, then handed him a tiny purse that he assumed—hoped—was Billie's.

The music screeched. Or maybe that was just the sounds the shocked people made as he passed them by.

He didn't know if he ought to be grateful or disgusted that nobody tried to stop him. But then, he thought about the last time he'd been in that very bar. The night before he'd gone out house-hunting with Billie that first time. The topless woman. The cops.

Maybe his hauling Billie out the way she was wasn't so shocking, after all.

He'd seen her car parked in the lot, but he didn't head toward it. Instead, he dumped her on the front seat of his pickup truck and tossed the tiny purse onto her lap.

She crossed her arms and glared at him. "If you were trying to embarrass me in front of my friends, you did a smashing job of it."

"Some friends. They didn't make a move to stop me. What're you doing in a place like that, anyway? It's a meat market."

"Maybe I was hungry!"

"And maybe you should be a vegetarian after all." Because he wasn't sure that she'd do it for herself, he strapped the safety belt across her chest and clipped it in place. When he started to straighten, he hesitated, his mouth close to hers. She smelled like wine and temptation.

He straightened and slammed the door shut. Rounded the truck and got behind the wheel.

At least she hadn't tried to bolt when she'd had the opportunity.

"If you think I'm going to let you tuck me in," she said when he started the engine, "you've got another think coming."

He ignored her and worked his way into the traffic surrounding the popular club. Instead of heading toward her apartment building, though, he headed to the highway.

He knew she realized it when she stiffened. "I don't know where you think you're taking me, but you can just turn this truck around right now."

"We're going home."

She snorted. "Your home? And do what? Sit down on the floor and drink tea from invisible cups?"

He ignored that, too, picking up speed as the traffic thinned a little.

She huffed and turned to look out the side window. They'd gone about ten miles when she finally spoke again. "You got a new cast."

"Yep."

"Suppose you'll ruin that one, too, soon enough."

"Probably."

She fell silent again.

His radio was turned off. The only sound was the lull of his steel-belted radials against the road.

"You hear that hum?"

Billie grunted. Not exactly an answer, but he decided to take it as one.

"It's a sound I'm comfortable with. The sound of most of my adult life, spent on the road, traveling from one rodeo to the next." His thumb tapped nervously against the steering wheel. He glanced at Billie. At the faint gleam of the three earrings on the upper curve of her sexy ear. "And now I'm looking at changing all that."

She was still. Not responding.

He could deal with that. Figured he more than deserved it, considering how he'd treated her in Paseo that last day. "I always thought my roots ran really deep in Paseo. But…" He shook his head. "They're not. Not like they are for Jayden and Nate." Just like when they'd both gone into the military the second they'd been able to, his course was taking a different route. A route that kept bringing him back to Billie.

"I need to put down new roots," he admitted. And even having rehearsed it more than once on the long drive from Paseo to Austin, he found his throat still felt tight around the words. "I've already got the lucky house. The only thing I need now is the reason it's lucky at all. You."

She didn't answer.

He stifled an oath. "You're gonna make me beg, aren't you?" He'd reached the turnoff for the ranch and he slowed. "Fine. I'll beg. But I'm not gonna apologize for not sleeping with you in Paseo. Sex has always been too easy for me. And whether you want to hear it or not, you started to mean more to me than that."

He parked in front of the house. "Dammit, Billie. Say something, even if it's telling me to go to hell." He touched her arm.

She finally moved, her head turning his way.

She was sound asleep.

Snoring slightly, even.

"Well. *Hell.*" Shows what he knew about women. Pouring his heart out while she quietly passed out on probably two glasses of wine.

He turned off the engine and got out of the truck, leaving the headlights on to see his way up to the front door and unlock it.

There wasn't any furniture inside the house. But he always had his bedroll in the truck.

When he checked Billie, she'd shucked off her seat belt and snuggled down in the seat, her cheek pressed against her clasped hands. Looking about sixteen, except for the long, shapely legs on display.

He reminded himself that he wasn't low enough to take advantage of an inebriated woman—even if he did love her—and grabbed the bedroll from the back seat. He carried it into the house, flipping on a couple lights as he made his way up to the master bedroom.

There, he spread out the bedroll, right where their real bed would someday be, and went back out to the truck.

She still hadn't moved.

His leg was aching from all the activity—just as the orthopedist had warned—but he ignored it and lifted Billie into his arms. No fireman's hold this time.

He cradled her against his chest and shoved the truck door closed with his shoulder. He didn't worry about the headlights. They'd turn off automatically before long.

He carried her inside the house, then up the stairs and to the bedroll. Lowering her onto it took some doing considering the immobility of his left leg in the boot. But he managed.

Her long hair slid over his arms and she sighed, one hand slipping around his neck. "Where're we?"

He smiled slightly and kissed her forehead. Her nose. Her lips. "We're home, sweetheart."

He hadn't turned on a light in the bedroom, but there was enough moonlight shining through the big windows to see that her eyes were open. Dark and gleaming.

He stretched out next to her and propped himself up on one arm. "Are you awake this time?"

"This time?"

He ran his fingers through her silky hair. He leaned down and brushed his lips against her triplet earrings. "How much did you have to drink?"

"A glass and a half of wine, smart aleck."

"Smart aleck, nothin'. You're the one who passed out on me in the truck. If I'm gonna pour my heart out to you, I'd like to know you're conscious enough to hear it." He propped himself on his arm again.

"You don't pour your heart out to anyone. You flirt."

"I'm not flirting now." He discarded the rehearsed speech and just pulled the ring out of his pocket. The ring he'd chosen that afternoon, after the orthopedist and before the autographing. "I love you, Billie Pemberton. Have pretty much loved you since that first day when you rescued me from cucumber-and-basil-poisoned water. And the deal was sealed for good when I woke up in the hospital with you crying by my side."

Her lashes dipped. He saw the gleam of a tear on her cheek and his chest tightened all over again as he gently thumbed it away. "If you marry me, I promise that I'll love you harder than anyone else ever could. But you need to understand that *you* are the catch. Not me. I'm just an old bulldogger with no chance of another championship this year, if ever. I've got a chip on my shoulder when it comes to my…when it comes to Gerald. Or Jerome. Or whoever the hell he is. And even though I've got a business with an office, I can guarantee that there are gonna be days when I want to still be on the road. Listening to the hum of the tires, going from rodeo to rodeo. Whether I can compete or not. It's just a part of who I am, sweetheart, and—"

Her fingertips touched his lips. "You love me?"

He caught her fingers in his hand and kissed them. And because she still hadn't said yes, he simply pushed the diamond ring on her finger. She'd either let it stay there for the rest of her life or he'd spend the rest of his life talking her into it. Either way, he wasn't taking it back. "I said so, didn't I? Do you want me to say it again?"

She nodded. "Again." She lifted herself up and kissed him slowly. "And again." Then she pushed on his shoulders until he rolled onto his back. She slid over him. "And again. Every morning." She pulled her short dress up and over her head and let it fall from her fingertips with a soft slithering sound. Her creamy shoulders gleamed in the moonlight. "And every night." She unclipped the wisp of lace that masqueraded as a bra and let that, too, fall to the side.

Then she leaned forward, cupping his face between her hands. "Can you handle that, Grayson Fortune?"

He grasped her hips, dipping his fingers beneath the flimsy sides of her skimpy panties. "S'long as you agree to become Billie Fortune." He slipped his hand between her thighs and couldn't help groaning when he found her wet heat.

Her breathing deepened. "Belinda Marie Fortune, if— ah—" She arched against his hand and started fumbling with his belt. "If we're going to be strictly accurate."

"By all means." He caught her lips with his. "Let's be strictly accurate." Before she could get too far, he flipped her until she was on her back. He peeled her panties the rest of the way down her smooth thighs, thoroughly exploring every inch of skin along the way. Until she was writhing against him far more enticingly than anything she'd done on the dance floor at Twine.

This dance was strictly for him.

He didn't have a hope in hell of quickly undoing the complicated straps holding the molded boot around his broken leg. "We were supposed to be doing this with *you* wearing the shoes," he murmured, as he pulled off his shirt, only to suck in a hard breath when her fingers trailed down his abdomen.

"Next time," she whispered huskily, peeling open his fly to work her hand inside his jeans.

He nearly came unglued. "There's a condom in my pocket," he said with a rough laugh.

"Engagement rings *and* condoms. The things you carry with you."

"I won't lie. The condoms were routine." He tried to put on the brakes. But her fingers were circled around him. Drawing him to her. Brakes were child's play. "The ring's a first."

"That's good. I want something to be a first for you." She slid her legs along his thighs, taking him in with a quick arching movement.

His heart nearly jumped out of his chest. He hadn't had sex without protection, ever. "You're on the Pill?"

She shook her head and brushed her lips over his. "Not since I was twenty."

"Holy—" He kissed her hard. "The toe tattoo guy was the last time?"

"Mmm." The tip of her tongue flirted along the edge of his ear. "Was no need after that. Don't worry. I'm perfectly safe. No dreaded diseases." She undulated against him, letting out a low, shaking sigh that was so erotic he had to count backward in his head just to keep some control.

"I'm safe, too," he managed to tell her. "But what if—"

"What if?" She was panting harder, her hands racing

from his hips, up his spine and back again. "You want to plant roots? Plant the first one now. Right now. With me."

His head went still, even though the rest of him was set on pursuing perfection inside her. "You were listening."

She twined her arms around his shoulders. "I was listening." Then she kissed him again. Tasting like wine and seduction and forever, while her body tightened so sweetly, so responsively, he couldn't do anything but rush headlong into the waves of her splintering around him.

The sun was coming up over the lake when Grayson next had a coherent thought.

He looked at Billie lying beside him and woke her with a kiss on her shoulder. "You never did say yes," he murmured.

She turned on her side, snuggling back against his chest and pulling his hand over her waist. "Maybe I'm still thinking about it."

He laughed and lightly swatted her bare butt.

Billie giggled, feeling happiness flood through her as she kissed his knuckles. "Yes. That doesn't, however, mean I'm waiving any of my commission when I find Grayson Gear's new corporate home. I mean, I'm not a pushover like someone I know."

"I'm not a pushover."

"Please." She twisted in his embrace and looped her arms around his neck. "You, who never met a cause he could resist? Admit it. The only real reason you want to make money at all is so that you can give it away to someone who needs it. It's one of the things I love most about you. That big, squishy heart of yours."

He made a face. "I like my comforts, too, sweetheart. The Harmon ranch? That's a lot of evidence."

"You would've been just as happy with the Orchess place. Half the price."

"Half the land," he countered immediately. "And no wine cellar where I can make love with my new fiancée. Speaking of which." He pushed to his knees and then to his feet. She'd helped him get rid of the rigid boot and his jeans before they'd made love a second time, and the sight of him in the dawn light was enough to make her catch her breath.

He was perfection personified.

"The wine cellar? Now?" She laughed softly as he limped into one of the large walk-in closets. "Pretty sure there isn't a secret staircase leading down there from the master bedroom closet, Grayson." But curiosity got the better of her when he didn't respond. The white shirt he'd been wearing the night before was lying in a heap next to the blanket he'd rolled out on the carpet, and she slipped her arms into it before heading after him.

If there'd been any shred of her heart that wasn't already melted into a Grayson puddle, it would have melted then.

He smiled at her, his rumpled hair sticking out around his handsome face. "What d'you think?"

She walked into the oversize closet. Slowly took the red-soled apology shoes off the fancy, lighted shelf where they'd been displayed. "You kept them."

"Only because every time I tried to get rid of them, they kept ending up right back in my possession. Reminding me of you. You still want to return them?"

She shook her head, set the shoes on the floor and slid her bare feet into them. They fit just as perfectly now as they had the first time he'd tempted her into trying them on.

"Come on, Billie. Tell me what you're thinking."

She smiled slowly. "Hopefully, the same thing you're thinking." She slid his shirt off her shoulders again and held out her arms to him. "That you have another promise to keep."

His smile was slow. Not at all trademark Grayson. But entirely *her* Grayson.

For now. And forever.

Epilogue

"You may kiss your bride."

Laughter and cheers followed, as the groom's handsome head lowered to his beautiful bride's and the two kissed. Probably a little longer than some might think appropriate.

Billie couldn't help but grin.

Lady Whatsername was now Mrs. Orlando Mendoza and Billie was pretty sure a bride had never looked as happy as Josephine Fortune Chesterfield did.

She leaned her head closer to Ariana, who was sitting beside her on the white chairs set up in pristine order among the ornamental grapevines at the Mendoza Winery. "Did you ever figure out just how they're all related?"

Ariana shrugged slightly. "I started a family chart once when I was planning to write the book about the Fortunes, but I gave up. Too complicated."

Grayson's hand covered Billie's. "We could have our wedding here at the winery, too," he murmured from the side of his mouth.

She shook her head. "We may not have agreed on a date yet, but we *have* agreed to have our wedding at home." Their home. Where they definitely wouldn't be having as large a guest list as Orlando and Josephine did, even though the Fortune ranch could have probably accommodated it.

There were almost as many people here now as when Schuyler had married Carlo. All the Mendozas who'd been present then were back. And there were Josephine's children from her prior marriages, as well as their spouses and their children. Plus Orlando's daughter and sons and all their families.

To say it was a huge crowd was putting it mildly.

Even when the wedding itself broke up and people started milling about as waiters circulated, bearing hot and cold hors d'oeuvres, the size of the guest list seemed to be one of the favorite topics. Either that or the designer duds that the bride and her daughters were sporting.

And Schuyler was clearly in her element in the winery as she flitted around, making certain that everyone had their glasses and plates filled. That everyone knew everyone else.

Billie was glad that there was at least one person not present. There was no sign whatsoever of Gerald Robinson, even though several of his children—Grayson, Jayden and Nathan aside—were present. But Deborah also had chosen to forgo the wedding, and Billie knew that Grayson feared the absence was too coincidental. He was clearly anxious to get away from all these people with whom he was even tenuously connected.

All she could do was hope that he'd be more accepting of his Fortune ties when they started *their* family.

He seemed to read her mind. "We can sneak out anytime you want," he murmured.

"Oh no, you don't," Schuyler said, overhearing as she personally topped off their glasses of champagne. "Not before the toasts at any rate." Her smile sparkled as she moved away.

Grayson looked pained. Billie knew it wouldn't be because of his leg. He was supposed to use a cane for the next two weeks. But of course, he wouldn't. "How long is this thing gonna last?"

Billie chuckled. "Hopefully not as long as Schuyler and Carlo's wedding did. I caught the bouquet. Well, half of it, anyway." She scanned the faces of the bridal couple's families and friends. "Wonder who'll catch Josephine's bouquet."

"Wonder if anyone cares?"

Billie bumped his arm. "Hush." Standing on the other side of Grayson, his brothers covered their smiles, and she gave them both a look. "You're not helping."

"Give up," Ariana advised. "When the three of them get going…" She shook her head. "No way of stopping." She hushed when Orlando and Josephine stepped onto a small dais near the winery entrance.

The couple held hands. "We're not going to stand up here and make long speeches," Orlando said. He smiled self-deprecatingly. "At least I won't subject you to mine. My wife, on the other hand—" he kissed the back of Josephine's fingers "—is much more graceful in front of a crowd than I." He shared a smile with his elegant bride. "I'll keep it short."

He held up his glass. "I wish for all of you to be as sheltered by love as we are today by your presence with us. People say you toast the bride and groom. But I say that we toast all of you." He raised his glass. "Cheers."

The sentiment resounded throughout the room as glasses clinked and people drank.

"And now, as promised, I will put a lock on it." Orlando mimed locking his lips together. Even across the distance, Billie could see the smile in the man's eyes.

"My new husband exaggerates greatly," Josephine said in her crisp British tones. "And I love him for it, particularly when he tells me I am more beautiful than the sea."

Orlando laughed and Josephine smiled. She definitely was comfortable in front of the large crowd. "I think we can all agree that the Fortune families and the Mendoza families have a long, storied history together," she said. "Some of our stories are longer. Some are shorter." She lifted her glass toward her groom. "But each is special. And unique. And joined by love. And I am so very grateful that I have been welcomed by all of you. As so many of us have learned, there is nothing more important than family."

Billie's eyes blurred a little. She reached out and found Grayson's hand with her own.

"Whether it's the family you've been born into or the family you've chosen, it all boils down to one thing. Hold on to those who love you. And let them hold on to you." She raised her glass one more time. "To all of you. Our family. Thank you for making this day even more special for us by taking the time to be here."

Ariana swiped at her eyes with the edge of her cocktail napkin. "Sheesh," she whispered, sharing a look with Billie. "Tear fest."

"And now, I, too, will be quiet," Josephine said with a soft laugh, "so we can get on with the food!"

Carlo walked to the front of the dais. It wasn't entirely

surprising, though Billie had sort of expected Alejandro—
Orlando's son—to speak. "Actually, there's just one more
thing we want to say before we begin this party in earnest." He nodded toward his uncle. "If you'll forgive me
hijacking the schedule for a moment."

Bianca looked at Billie. Her eyes were dancing. "Ten
to one, Schuyler's pregnant."

Billie wasn't going to take that bet. Because she'd immediately thought the same thing. And when Schuyler
stepped beside Carlo and took his hand, she was certain of it.

"I'm glad that my new aunt-in-law spoke about the
importance of family," she said. "Because there's actually more family here than any of you know."

"When's the due date?" someone called out.

Schuyler laughed and propped her hand on her spectacular skin-hugging dress. "Now, y'all. Seriously. Do I
look pregnant?" She grinned. "Carlo and I have lots of
time to make babies."

Billie caught the way Carlo squeezed her hand encour-
agingly. *"Go ahead,"* she saw him mouth.

"Actually…" She took a deep breath and let it out in
an audible rush. "It's me. And my brothers and my sisters. We were born Fortunados. But under that, we're
Fortunes, same as a lot of you. Our daddy's daddy was
Julius Fortune, Jerome's father." She suddenly looked toward where Grayson and they all stood. "Same as your
granddaddy." She looked over to Alejandro and his wife,
Olivia Robinson Mendoza. "And same as *your* granddaddy." She spread her arms wide. "And *boy* is it a load
off my chest to finally admit it to y'all!"

Far from looking upset, Josephine merely stepped off
the dais and hugged Schuyler. "Once again," she said, so
brightly that people laughed rather than gasped, "there's

simply no end to this dynasty. Mark my words, we need a Fortune family reunion—"

"Fortune family meet-and-greet," someone called out with a laugh.

Josephine's smile widened. "—and soon!"

Grayson wasn't laughing, though. "Are we sure that there aren't cousins marrying cousins or something?"

Ariana heard him. "Fortunately, back when I was trying to map it all out, none of that ever happened."

"Small wonder." He looked around them. "Any other secrets coming out today?"

"Just one." Billie knew one sure way to clear the discontented look from Grayson's face. "Maybe Schuyler's not pregnant, but—" she shrugged slightly and met his eyes "—I am."

His jaw dropped. "It hasn't been that long since—" He broke off. Swallowed. "How do you know?" He swept his hands down the sides of her purple dress. The fact that they weren't exactly steady made her love him all the more. "Are you sure?"

"The home test I did seemed pretty sure."

He threw back his head. Let out a whoop and lifted her right off her feet, swinging her in a circle. "Sweetheart, I don't care what you say." He set her back on her feet. "We are out of here." He grabbed her hand and pulled her past the ornamental vines.

"And that there's Grayson, folks." Jayden's pseudo-rodeo announcer's voice followed them. "Breaking yet another timed record…this one the fastest wedding exit ever!"

Laughing breathlessly as they raced across the green, green grass, Billie pulled on Grayson's hand to stop him. "You're really okay with this?"

His eyes softened. "Planting roots with you? Belinda

Marie soon-to-be Fortune, don't you know the truth by now?" His hands cupped her face. "*You* are my forever home."

Her eyes flooded. She didn't think her heart could be filled any more, but it was. "Grayson."

His eyes weren't exactly dry then, either. "*Now* can we get outta here and go set a dang wedding date? We've gotta tell your folks. Tell my mom. Sweetheart, there's stuff to be done!"

She laughed. Leaned down to slip off her red-soled shoes, then she held out her free hand to him. "Let's go."

He closed his hand around hers. And they went.

* * * * *

Don't miss the FORTUNES OF TEXAS
holiday special,
FORTUNE'S CHRISTMAS BABY
by USA TODAY *bestselling author*
Tara Taylor Quinn

Coming in December 2018!

And catch up with
THE FORTUNES OF TEXAS:
THE RULEBREAKERS

Look for:

HER SOLDIER OF FORTUNE by
Michelle Major

NO ORDINARY FORTUNE by
USA TODAY *bestselling author Judy Duarte*

THE FORTUNE MOST LIKELY TO...
by USA TODAY *bestselling author*
Marie Ferrarella

FORTUNE'S FAMILY SECRETS
by USA TODAY *bestselling author*
Karen Rose Smith

MADDIE FORTUNE'S PERFECT MAN
by Nancy Robards Thompson

and

FORTUNE'S HOMECOMING by
New York Times *bestselling author Allison Leigh*

Available now, wherever Harlequin books
and ebooks are sold.

Keep reading for a special preview of
HERONS LANDING,
the first in an exciting new series from
New York Times *bestselling author*
JoAnn Ross and HQN Books!

CHAPTER ONE

SETH HARPER WAS spending a Sunday spring afternoon detailing his wife's Rallye Red Honda Civic when he learned that she'd been killed by a suicide bomber in Afghanistan.

Despite the Pacific Northwest's reputation for unrelenting rain, the sun was shining so brightly that the Army notification officers—a man and a woman in dark blue uniforms and black shoes spit-shined to a mirror gloss—had been wearing shades. Or maybe, Seth considered, as they'd approached the driveway in what appeared to be slow motion, they would've worn them anyway. Like armor, providing emotional distance from the poor bastard whose life they were about to blow to smithereens.

At the one survivor grief meeting he'd later attended (only to get his fretting mother off his back), he'd heard stories from other spouses who'd experienced a sudden, painful jolt of loss before their official notice. Seth hadn't received any advance warning. Which was why, at first, the officers' words had been an incomprehensible buzz in his ears. Like distant radio static.

Zoe couldn't be dead. His wife wasn't a combat soldier. She was an Army surgical nurse, working in a heavily protected military base hospital, who'd be returning to civilian life in two weeks. Seth still had a bunch of stuff on his homecoming punch list to do. After buffing the wax off the Civic's hood and shining up the chrome wheels, his next project was to paint the walls white in the nursery he'd added on to their Folk Victorian cottage for the baby they'd be making.

She'd begun talking a lot about baby stuff early in her deployment. Although Seth was as clueless as the average guy about a woman's mind, it didn't take Dr. Phil to realize that she was using the plan to start a family as a touchstone. Something to hang on to during their separation.

In hours of Skype calls between Honeymoon Harbor and Kabul, they'd discussed the pros and cons of the various names on a list that had grown longer each time they'd talked. While the names remained up in the air, she *had* decided that whatever their baby's gender, the nursery should be a bright white to counter the Olympic Peninsula's gray skies.

She'd also sent him links that he'd dutifully followed to Pinterest pages showing bright crib bedding, mobiles and wooden name letters in primary crayon shades of blue, green, yellow and red. Even as Seth had lobbied for Seattle Seahawk navy and action green, he'd known that he'd end up giving his wife whatever she wanted.

The same as he'd been doing since the day he fell head over heels in love with her back in middle school.

Meanwhile, planning to get started on that baby making as soon as she got back to Honeymoon Harbor, he'd built the nursery as a welcome-home surprise.

Then Zoe had arrived at Sea-Tac Airport in a flag-draped casket.

And two years after the worst day of his life, the room remained unpainted behind a closed door Seth had never opened since.

MANNION'S PUB & BREWERY was located on the street floor of a faded redbrick building next to Honeymoon Harbor's ferry landing. The former salmon cannery had been one of many buildings constructed after the devastating 1893 fire that had swept along the waterfront, burning down the original wood buildings. One of Seth's ancestors, Jacob Harper, had built the replacement in 1894 for the town's mayor and pub owner, Finn Mannion. Despite the inability of Washington authorities to keep Canadian alcohol from flooding into the state, the pub had been shuttered during Prohibition in the 1930s, effectively putting the Mannions out of the pub business until Quinn Mannion had returned home from Seattle and hired Harper Construction to reclaim the abandoned space.

Although the old Victorian seaport town wouldn't swing into full tourist mode until Memorial Day, nearly every table was filled when Seth dropped in at the end of the day. He'd no sooner slid onto a stool at the end of the long wooden bar when Quinn, who'd been washing glasses in a sink, stuck a bottle of Shipwreck CDA in front of him.

"Double cheddar bacon or stuffed blue cheese?" he asked.

"Double cheddar bacon." As he answered the question, it crossed Seth's mind that his life—what little he had outside his work of restoring the town's Victorian buildings constructed by an earlier generation of Harpers—had possibly slid downhill beyond routine to boringly predictable. "And don't bother boxing it up. I'll be eating it here," he added.

Quinn lifted a dark brow. "I didn't see that coming."

Meaning that, by having dinner here at the pub six nights a week, the seventh being with Zoe's parents—where they'd recount old memories, and look through scrapbooks of photos that continued to cause an ache deep in his heart—he'd undoubtedly landed in the predictable zone. So, what was wrong with that? Predictability was an underrated concept. By definition, it meant a lack of out-of-the-blue surprises that might destroy life as you knew it. Some people might like change. Seth was not one of them. Which was why he always ordered takeout with his first beer of the night.

The second beer he drank at home with his burger and fries. While other guys in his position might have escaped reality by hitting the bottle, Seth always stuck to a limit of two bottles, beginning with that long, lonely dark night after burying his wife. Because, although he'd never had a problem with alcohol, he harbored a secret fear that if he gave in to the temptation to begin seriously drinking, he might never stop.

The same way if he ever gave in to the anger, the unfairness of what the hell had happened, he'd have to patch a lot more walls in his house than he had those first few months after the notification officers' arrival.

There'd been times when he'd decided that someone in the Army had made a mistake. That Zoe hadn't died at all. Maybe she'd been captured during a melee and no one knew enough to go out searching for her. Or perhaps she was lying in some other hospital bed, her face all bandaged, maybe with amnesia, or even in a coma, and some lab tech had mixed up blood samples with another soldier who'd died. That could happen, right?

But as days slid into weeks, then weeks into months, he'd come to accept that his wife really was gone. Most of the time. Except when he'd see her, from behind, strolling down the street, window-shopping or walking onto the ferry, her dark curls blowing into a frothy tangle. He'd embarrassed himself a couple times by calling out her name. Now he never saw her at all. And worse yet, less and less in his memory. Zoe was fading away. Like that ghost who reputedly haunted Herons Landing, the old Victorian mansion up on the bluff overlooking the harbor.

"I'm having dinner with Mom tonight." And had been dreading it all the damn day. Fortunately, his dad hadn't heard about it yet. But since news traveled at the speed of sound in Honeymoon Harbor, he undoubtedly soon would.

"You sure you don't want to wait to order until she gets here?"

"She's not eating here. It's a command-performance dinner," he said. "To have dinner with her and the guy who may be her new boyfriend. Instead of eating at her new apartment, she decided that it'd be better to meet on neutral ground."

"Meaning somewhere other than a brewpub owned and operated by a Mannion," Quinn said. "Especially given the rumors that said new boyfriend just happens to be my uncle Mike."

"That does make the situation stickier." Seth took a long pull on the Cascadian Dark Ale and wished it was something stronger.

The feud between the Harpers and Mannions dated back to the early 1900s. After having experienced a boom during the end of the nineteenth century, the once-bustling seaport town had fallen on hard times during a national financial depression.

Although the population declined drastically, those dreamers who'd remained were handed a stroke of luck in 1910 when the newlywed king and queen of Montacroix added the town to their honeymoon tour of America. The couple had learned of this lush green region from the king's friend Theodore Roosevelt, who'd set aside national land for the Mount Olympus Monument.

As a way of honoring the royals, and hoping that the national and European press following them across the country might bring more attention to the town, residents had voted nearly unanimously to change the name to Honeymoon Harbor. Seth's ancestor Nathaniel Harper had been the lone holdout, creating acrimony on both sides that continued to linger among some but not all of the citizens. Quinn's father, after all, was a Mannion, his mother a Harper. But Ben Harper, Seth's father, tended to nurse his grudges. Even century-old ones that had nothing to do with him. Or at least hadn't. Until lately.

"And it gets worse," he said.

"Okay."

One of the things that made Quinn such a good bartender was that he listened a lot more than he talked. Which made Seth wonder how he'd managed to spend all those years as a big-bucks corporate lawyer in Seattle before returning home to open this pub and microbrewery.

"The neutral location she chose is Leaf."

Quinn's quick laugh caused two women who were drinking wine at a table looking out over the water to glance up with interest. Which wasn't surprising. Quinn's brother, Wall Street wizard Gabe Mannion, might be richer, New York City pro quarterback Burke Mannion flashier, and, last time he'd seen him, which had admittedly been a while, Marine-turned-LA-cop Aiden Mannion had still carried that bad-boy vibe that had gotten him in trouble a lot while they'd been growing up together. But Quinn's superpower had always been the ability to draw the attention of females—from bald babies in strollers to blue-haired elderly women in walkers—without seeming to do a thing.

After turning in the burger order, and helping out his waitress by delivering meals to two of the tables, Quinn returned to the bar and began hanging up the glasses.

"Let me guess," he said. "You ordered the burger as an appetizer before you go off to a vegetarian restaurant to dine on alfalfa sprouts and pretty flowers."

"It's a matter of survival. I spent the entire day until I walked in here taking down a wall, adding a new reinforcing beam and framing out a bathroom. A guy needs sustenance. Not a plate of arugula and pansies."

"Since I run a place that specializes in pub grub, you're not going to get any argument from me on that plan. Do you still want the burger to go for the mutt?"

Bandit, a black Lab/boxer mix so named for his penchant for stealing food from Seth's construction sites back in his stray days—including once gnawing through a canvas ice chest—usually waited patiently in the truck for his burger. Tonight Seth had dropped him off at the house on his way over here, meaning the dog would have to wait a little longer for his dinner. Not that he hadn't mooched enough from the framers already today. If the vet hadn't explained strays' tendencies for overeating because they didn't know where their next meal might be coming from, Seth might have suspected the street-scarred dog he'd rescued of having a tapeworm.

They shot the breeze while Quinn served up drinks,

which in this place ran more to the craft beer he brewed in the building next door. A few minutes later, the swinging door to the kitchen opened and out came two layers of prime beef topped with melted local cheddar cheese, bacon and caramelized grilled onions, with a slice of tomato and an iceberg-lettuce leaf tossed in as an apparent nod to the food pyramid, all piled between the halves of an oversize toasted kaiser bun. Taking up the rest of the heated metal platter was a mountain of spicy french fries.

Next to the platter was a take-out box of plain burger. It wouldn't stay warm, but having first seen the dog scrounging from a garbage can on the waterfront, Seth figured Bandit didn't care about the temperature of his dinner.

"So, you're eating in tonight," a bearded giant wearing a T-shirt with Embrace the Lard on the front said in a deep foghorn voice. "I didn't see that coming."

"Everyone's a damn joker," Seth muttered, even as the aroma of grilled beef and melted cheese drew him in. He took a bite and nearly moaned. The Norwegian, who'd given up cooking on fishing boats when he'd gotten tired of freezing his ass off during winter crabbing season, might be a sarcastic smart-ass, but the guy sure as hell could cook.

"He's got a dinner date tonight at Leaf." Quinn, for some damn reason, chose this moment to decide to get chatty. "This is an appetizer."

Jarle Bjornstad snorted. "I tried going vegan," he said. "I'd hooked up with a woman in Anchorage who wouldn't even wear leather. It didn't work out."

"Mine's not that kind of date." Seth wondered how much arugula, kale and flowers it would take to fill up the man with shoulders as wide as a redwood trunk and arms like huge steel bands. His full-sleeve tattoo boasted a butcher's chart of a cow. Which might explain his ability to turn a beef patty into something close to nirvana. "And there probably aren't enough vegetables on the planet to sustain you."

During the remodeling, Seth had taken out four rows of bricks in the wall leading to the kitchen to allow the six-foot-seven-inch-tall cook to go back and forth without having to duck his head to keep from hitting the doorjamb every trip.

"On our first date, she cited all this damn research claiming vegans lived nine years longer than meat eaters." Jarle's teeth flashed in a grin in his flaming red beard. "After a week of grazing, I decided that her statistics might be true, but that extra time would be nine horrible baconless years."

That said, he turned and stomped back into the kitchen.

"He's got a point," Quinn said.

"Amen to that." Having learned firsthand how treacherous and unpredictable death could be, with his current family situation on the verge of possibly exploding, Seth decided to worry about his arteries later and took another huge bite of beef-and-cheese heaven.

Need to know what happens next?
Order your copy of HERONS LANDING
wherever you buy your books!

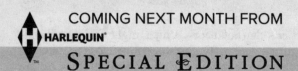
#2629 A MAVERICK TO (RE)MARRY
Montana Mavericks: The Lonelyhearts Ranch • by Christine Rimmer
Not only were Derek Dalton and Amy Wainwright once an item, they were actually married! With Amy back in town for her friend's wedding, how long before their secret past is revealed?

#2630 DETECTIVE BARELLI'S LEGENDARY TRIPLETS
The Wyoming Multiples • by Melissa Senate
Norah Ingalls went to bed a single mom of triplets—and woke up married! They might try to blame it on the spiked punch, but Detective Reed Barelli is finding it impossible to walk away from this instant family!

#2631 HOW TO ROMANCE A RUNAWAY BRIDE
Wilde Hearts • by Teri Wilson
Days before she turns thirty, Allegra Clark finds herself a runaway bride! Lucky for her, she accidentally crashes a birthday party for Zander Wilde— the man who promised to marry her if neither of them was married by thirty...

#2632 THE SOLDIER'S TWIN SURPRISE
Rocking Chair Rodeo • by Judy Duarte
Erica Campbell is only here to give army pilot Clay Matthews the news: she's having his babies. Two of them! But can she count on Clay—a man whose dreams of military glory have just been dashed—to be her partner in parenthood?

#2633 THE SECRET SON'S HOMECOMING
The Cedar River Cowboys • by Helen Lacey
Jonah Rickard, the illegitimate son of J. D. O'Sullivan, wants nothing to do with his "other" family. Unfortunately, he's falling for Connie Bedford, who's practically part of the family, and he'll have to confront his past to claim the future he wants.

#2634 THE CAPTAIN'S BABY BARGAIN
American Heroes • by Merline Lovelace
After one hot night, Captain Suzanne Hall remembers everything she craved about her sexy ex-husband. Now she's pregnant and Gabe thinks they should get married...again! Will they be able to overcome everything that tore them apart before?

Get 4 FREE REWARDS!

We'll send you 2 FREE Books
<u>plus</u> 2 FREE Mystery Gifts.

Harlequin® Special Edition
books feature heroines
finding the balance
between their work life
and personal life on the
way to finding true love.

FREE
Value Over
$20

Is that what you want? The question was still there, in his
eyes. All she had to do was decide.

She took a deep breath and shook her head.

Zander leaned closer, his eyes hard on hers. Then he
reached to cup her face with his free hand and drew the
pad of his thumb slowly, deliberately along the swell of
her bottom lip. "Tell me what you want, Allegra."

You. She swallowed. *I want you.*

"This," she said, reaching up on tiptoe to close the
space between them and touch her lips to his.

What are you doing? Stop.

But it was too late to change her mind. Too late to
pretend she didn't want this. Because the moment her
mouth grazed Zander's, he took ownership of the kiss.

His hands slid into her hair, holding her in place, while
his tongue slid brazenly along the seam of her lips until
they parted, opening for him.

Then there was nothing but heat and want and the
shocking reality that this was what she'd wanted all
along. Zander.

Had she always felt this way? It seemed impossible. Yet beneath the newness of his mouth on hers and the crush of her breasts against the solid wall of his chest, there was something else. A feeling she couldn't quite put her finger on. A sense of belonging. Of destiny.

Home.

Allegra squeezed her eyes closed. She didn't want to imagine herself fitting into this life again. There was too much at stake. Too much to lose. But no matter how hard she railed against it, there it was, shimmering before like her a mirage.

She whimpered into Zander's mouth, and he groaned in return, gently guiding her backward until her spine was pressed against the cool marble wall. Before she could register what was happening, he gathered her wrists and pinned them above her head with a single, capable hand. And the last remaining traces of resistance melted away. She couldn't fight it anymore. Not from this position of delicious surrender. Her arms went lax, and somewhere in the back of her mind, a wall came tumbling down.

The breath rushed from her body, and a memory came into focus with perfect, crystalline clarity.

Let's make a deal. If neither of us is married by the time we turn thirty, we'll marry each other. Agreed?

Agreed?

Don't miss
HOW TO ROMANCE A RUNAWAY BRIDE
by Teri Wilson, available July 2018 wherever
Harlequin® Special Edition books and ebooks are sold.

www.Harlequin.com

THE WORLD IS BETTER WITH

Romance

Harlequin has everything from contemporary, passionate and heartwarming to suspenseful and inspirational stories.

Whatever your mood, we have a romance just for you!

Connect with us to find your next great read, special offers and more.

f /HarlequinBooks

🐦 @HarlequinBooks

www.HarlequinBlog.com

www.Harlequin.com/Newsletters

HARLEQUIN®

A *Romance* FOR EVERY MOOD™

www.Harlequin.com

SERIESHALOAD2015